"DELPHI FABRICE" (the pseud[...] Henri-Adhémar Risselin, 1877-[...] literary career as an art critic w[...] *Bretagne* (1898), before becoming involved [...] Decadent Movement, under the aesthetic of which he composed a number of works, including *L'Araignée rouge* (1903), the one-act drama *Clair de lune* (1903), which was co-written with Jean Lorrain, Fabrice's mentor, and *La sorcier rouge* (1910). Under the need for money, he gradually turned his attention to romance novels, novels of adventure geared towards a juvenile audience, and "cine-novels" (adaptations of films into photo-novels). In all, he is credited with writing over 120 books.

BRIAN STABLEFORD'S scholarly work includes *New Atlantis: A Narrative History of Scientific Romance* (Wildside Press, 2016), *The Plurality of Imaginary Worlds: The Evolution of French roman scientifique* (Black Coat Press, 2017) and *Tales of Enchantment and Disenchantment: A History of Faerie* (Black Coat Press, 2019). In support of the latter projects he has translated more than a hundred volumes of *roman scientifique* and more than twenty volumes of *contes de fées* into English. His recent fiction, in the genre of metaphysical fantasy, includes a trilogy of novels set in West Wales, consisting of *Spirits of the Vasty Deep* (2018), *The Insubstantial Pageant* (2018) and *The Truths of Darkness* (2019), published by Snuggly Books, and a trilogy set in Paris and the south of France, consisting of *The Painter of Spirits*, *The Quiet Dead* and *Living with the Dead*, all published by Black Coat Press in 2019.

DELPHI FABRICE

FLOWERS
OF
ETHER

TRANSLATED AND WITH AN INTRODUCTION BY
BRIAN STABLEFORD

THIS IS A SNUGGLY BOOK

ISBN: 978-1-64525-070-8

CONTENTS

Introduction / *7*

Eyes of Faded Cornflower Blue / *21*
A Session with Wild Beasts / *27*
Her Advertisement! / *33*
The Man of Prey / *40*
The Amorous Woman of the River-Bank / *46*
The Lady of the Opals / *53*
The Man From Billancourt / *60*
A Woman's Vengeance / *66*
At the Pont d'Iéna / *71*
The Bizarre Adventure / *77*
His Mistress / *83*
Amorous Trinity / *93*
Gabrielle Mina / *100*
Prediction / *106*
The Matelot Reappears / *114*
A Corner of the Veil is Lifted / *120*
Toward the Sabbat! / *127*
The Froleuse / *133*
The House of a Hundred Eyes / *140*

An Evening of Poisons / *147*
A Nostalgic Soul / *153*
After the Sin / *160*
The End of the Orgy / *167*
Spiders of the Fortifs / *175*
The End of the Adventure / *182*

INTRODUCTION

"FLEURS D'ÉTHER ET DE TALUS" by Delphi Fabrice (the pseudonym of Gaston-Henri-Adhémar Risselin, 1877-1937), here translated as *Flowers of Ether*,[1] first appeared as a serial in the "literary supplement" of the daily newspaper *La Lanterne*, the episodes bearing that heading appearing at approximately weekly intervals between 17 January 1903 and 25 June 1903, although the series had actually begun under the heading "Nuits de Paris et ailleurs" in the 1 January 1903 issue of the supplement. It does not appear to have been reprinted in book form, although it is not impossible that it featured among the au-

---

1 I have abbreviated the title of the translation because the original is slightly enigmatic; if it had "*du talus*" rather than "*de talus*" it would obviously refer to the embankment of the old fortifications of Paris, to which Lorrain and Fabrice often referred as the "fortifs," some derelict sections of which had become notorious haunts of criminals and prostitutes by 1900—especially the fenced-off "waste ground" that had been scheduled for redevelopment and has now vanished from the Parisian landscape—but the actual form of the title implies "slope" in a more general, perhaps metaphorical, sense.

thor's prolific publications under a different title. Its serial publication overlapped the publication in book form of Fabrice's novel *L'Araignée rouge* (tr. as *The Red Spider*), in March 1903, the writing of which had probably been completed before the end of 1901, and which had been preceded by a play of the same title, prepared for production in 1900 before being banned by the censor. Like *L'Araignée rouge*, *Fleurs d'éther et de talus* is to some extent a gesture of defiance addressed to the censor, deliberately treating equivocal themes that could not yet be treated safely on stage and were a trifle risky in a daily newspaper.

The serial can be regarded as a sequel of sorts to the novel, although it cannot be taken entirely for granted that the unnamed narrator of the novel is the same person as the "Fabrice" who serves as the narrator of the serial. Nor can it be taken for granted that the "Fabrice" of the serial bears much resemblance to its author, "Delphi Fabrice"—itself a disguise of course—in spite of the obvious invitation to do so. The serial is not a *roman à clef*; the fictitious Jean des Glaïeuls [Jean of the Gladioli] is not a representation of Delphi Fabrice's friend and mentor Jean Lorrain, nor is the fictitious Nine d'Aubusson, Fabrice's interlocutor, the narrator of the principal story-within-the-story, a representation of Lorrain's one-time protégée Liane de Pougy, although the two characters reproduce a few features of those two real individuals, and there is an inevitable temptation to wonder whether their relationship with the Fabrice of the story might contain any echoes of the relationship between the real individuals and the actual author—a temptation that needs to be treated with the utmost caution, because, rather than in spite of its allure. The relationship between the fiction and reality is far more complicated than any simple mirroring.

Delphi Fabrice was born in Paris, but little else is recorded about his biography except for the data recorded on his birth certificate and the statements he made about himself in the introductions to his books, which are probably not reliable; although the present text is not the only one narrated by "Fabrice" it would be dangerous to assume that any of the statements made by "Fabrice" about himself—including his allegations of once-prolific use of ether, hashish and morphine—are applicable to the real author. No photographs of him are discoverable via the internet, nor is he identifiable in any of the caricatures by "Sem" (Georges Goursat, 1863-1934), whose annual "album" often featured Jean Lorrain, Liane de Pougy and other members of their briefly-prominent social circle. What is reliably known is the list of the publications he signed (occasionally under the easily-attributable pseudonym Fabrice Delphi), but although it is long, it does not include unbylined work for newspapers or any work "ghost-written" for publication under other signatures.

Fabrice first began publishing work in the mid-1890s, the first book he signed being a study of *Les Peintres de Bretagne* (1898), and it was in that period that he met and began working in association with Oscar Méténier, who founded the Grand-Guignol theater in 1897 but continued to support and supply material to other theaters; Fabrice collaborated with Méténier on various dramatic projects, and it was probably through him that he met Jean Lorrain, by then the figurehead and chief exemplar of the literary "Decadent Movement." The precise nature of the relationship between Fabrice and Lorrain is unknown, but they collaborated on several literary and theatrical projects, and Fabrice modeled his own literary endeavors very closely on Lorrain's for several years.

In the late 1890s Lorrain was a regular contributor to *Le Journal*, which then had a stable of writers producing fiction or articles on a weekly or fortnightly basis, generally used as the lead items on page one; he mingled his admittedly fictional contributions with items that masqueraded as non-fiction, in which he figured as a narrator. Lorrain also had a "diary column," signed "Raitif de la Bretonne" in honor of Nicolas Restif de La Bretonne's largely fictitious accounts of his supposed nocturnal wanderings in Paris, collected as *Nuits de Paris* (1788-94), which he imitated. Fabrice copied his idol faithfully in his own signed contributions to the literary supplement of the daily newspaper *La Lanterne*, which were a regular feature between 1902 and 1909, by which time the supplement in question, originally weekly, and then twice-weekly, was being published three times a week; some of his items of fake autobiography were collected in a curious pseudojournalistic account of *L'Opium à Paris* (1907), the most successful of his "non-fiction" books.

The extent of Fabrice's unbylined work for *La Lanterne* is incalculable, but he certainly made substantial contributions to one of the *Supplement's* two gossip columns, one of which was headed "Le Carnet de Lionnette" and sometimes signed "Mary Lionnette" and the other "Le Monsieur de chez Maxim" [The Man from Maxim's (Restaurant)] or simply headlined "Échos." In 1903 Fabrice sometimes added a by-line to selected items in the "Échos" column, either using his usual pseudonym or "Jean des Glaïeuls," the name of the imaginary author whose exploits form the substance of "Fleurs d'éther et de talus." That pseudonym was subsequently attached to a number of short stories in the *Supplement*, including the couplet "Les Débuts de Jane Vadrouille" (23 February 1905) and "Autre débuts" (2 March 1905).[1] The extent to which Fabrice's contributions to the gossip column and his fictional accounts of the seamier side of Parisian life were based on personal observation rather than recycling information fed to him by Méténier and Lorrain is also incalculable, but there is no doubt that Lorrain played a crucial role in the invisible part of his career

---

1 Other stories in *Le Supplement* signed "Jean des Glaïeuls" include "La Canne" (14 February 1905), "La Muselière" (20 April 1905), "Ton Rire" (20 February 1906), "Le Korrigan" (10 March 1906), "Le Bon trigame" (22 March 1906), "Les vêtements du petit tondu" (14 April 1906), "Le Misereux" (12 June 1906). "La Guigne du Maître de Bains" (7 July 1906), "Le Bon coiffeur" (21 July 1906), "La Voiture dangereuse" (23 August 1906), "La Voyageuese récalcitrante" (25 September 1906) and, belatedly, the three-part feuilleton "La Dame aux Opales," (3, 10 & 17 April 1920).

by introducing him to the notorious "courtesan" Liane de Pougy (1869-1950), with whom his collaboration on more than one theatrical piece was acknowledged and whom he surely served as a ghost-writer as well as a publicist.

Pougy's stage career—the Parisian stage in the Belle Époque, at all its many levels, was primarily a showcase for ambitious "trophy mistresses" to fish for suppliers of houses, carriages and jewels—was planned and guided by the self-styled Comtesse Valtesse de la Bigne, who had added a touch of class to her own career as a pretentious prostitute by publishing a supposedly autobiographical novel, and Pougy did the same. Pougy would undoubtedly have turned initially to Lorrain for help in that task, as he was playing a leading role in supplying her with free publicity in the newspapers, but it was probably inevitable that the ever-busy Lorrain would delegate the task to one of his acolytes; Fabrice might well have made a substantial uncredited contribution to Pougy's novels *L'Insaissable* (1898) and *Myrrhille* (1899), the subject-matter of which is echoed in several "courtesan novels" bearing his own signature. Both novels are calculatedly sensational but not as sensational as "Fleurs d'éther et de talus," whose title implies, unsubtly but not entirely accurately, that it is endeavoring to take such sensationalism to a new level.

Liane de Pougy followed up the first two novels bearing her signature with a *roman à clef,* two plays and two further items of supposed autobiography. *Idylle sapphique* (1901) is a disguised account of her seduction by the notorious lesbian Natalie Barney, an American socialite whose salon became the meeting-place of a coterie of talented female poets, including "Renée Vivien" (Pauline Tarn) and Lucie Delarue-Mardrus. It is markedly different from the account of lesbian seduction included in "Fleur d'éther et de talus," which is less coy in its description but serves nevertheless to cover up an inconvenient lacuna in its elliptical account of a troilistic orgy. The next quasi-autobiographical novel to be published under Pougy's signature was *Ecce homo: d'ici de là* (1903), which was rapidly followed by "Dix ans de fête: Mémoires d'une demi-mondaine," which began serialization in the *Lanterne Supplement* in November 1903. Although it only carried Pougy's byline it had been advertised as forthcoming in the "Échos" of the 28 July edition of the *Supplement* as a collaboration with Fabrice, represented there as a novel rather than an actual memoir, albeit with the emphatic statement that it was "*toujours vrais.*"[1]

---

1 Another item in that same gossip column is signed "Jean des Glaïeuls"; the same signature is appended to a curious letter addressed to Liane de Pougy in the "Échos" column of 26 May 1893 imploring her not to write any more plays after the recently-produced flop "L'Agonie;" only three days before, an unsigned piece in the column had reported that she had put forward her candidature for a vacant seat in the Académie française. The "Échos" column of 8 August includes another letter to Liane, this time signed "Delphi Fabrice," ostensibly sent while both were ill in bed (she might have been suffering from the aftermath of one of her several failed suicide attempts); it addresses her as "Liline" and refers to regular correspondence between them. The newspaper's theatrical columns of 6 and 9 July had related that she was taking the star role in a "pantomime" written especially

13

Just as the border between fact and fiction is extremely blurred in Liane de Pougy's supposed writings—and, for that matter, in her life—so Delphi Fabrice's writings, so far as they are known, often operate in a murky gray area of unreliable reportage. Was he really a reformed drug abuser and flamboyant homosexual poseur, like the Fabrice of "Fleurs d'éther et de talus"? One suspects not, but who can tell? The flamboyantly homosexual Jean Lorrain had given up ether-drinking some time before he wrote his *contes d'un buveur d'éther*, and although he did not want to shake off the reputation that they had cultivated for him, by 1903 he had adopted a much more moderate lifestyle—although the gossip column of *Le Supplement* dutifully reported on 28 April that he had escorted Liane de Pougy to a costume ball, both spectacularly travestied as vagabonds—and he had been living in Nice for three years with his mother, only making occasional trips to Paris. That did not prevent him from dying three years later of peritonitis, the same problem that the Fabrice of "Fleurs d'éther et de talus" claims to have imperiled his life. Other "decadent" writers also cultivated a reputation for drug abuse for the purposes of image maintenance, including Gabriel de Lautrec, to whom a disguised passing reference is made in "Fleurs d'éther et de talus," and Maurice Magre, who copied Fabrice's mock-journalistic study of *Opium in Paris* with a similar study of a secret underworld in *Magie à Paris* (1934, signed "René Thimmy").

for her by Fabrice and the actor and songwriter "Gardel-Hervé" (Louis Ronger, 1847-1926), which was produced as *Témoin*.

Whatever the reality might have been that lay behind "Fleurs d'éther et de talus," Fabrice did not make any further attempts to increase the stakes in pushing the envelope of excess. He was probably sobered up by cautionary advice like that given to Nina d'Aubusson in the story to beware of courting scandal too closely. Jean Lorrain was sued for libel after making too much use of personal knowledge in the story-series "Femmes" that ran in *Le Journal* while the *Supplement* was serializing "Fleurs d'éther et de talus," and the complainant, Jeanne Jacquemin—another of his former protégées—was awarded huge punitive damages, only belatedly cancelled on appeal. Also in 1903, in the newspaper rather than the literary supplement, *La Lanterne* devoted extensive publicity to the arrest, trial and attempted suicide of the homosexual writer Jacques Adelswärd, charged with "depraving youth" by hosting obscene parties featuring "living tableaux" of ephebes—which the gentlemen of the press, never reluctant to exaggerate, did not hesitate to describe as "black masses" as well as pederastic orgies. Jean Lorrain obligingly provided an analysis of his friend's "special psychology" to the *Lanterne* in August, but his efforts could not save him from eventual conviction. Adelswärd—subsequently known as Adelswärd-Fersen in order to emphasize his kinship with one of Marie-Antoinette's alleged lovers—was forced into exile from France, but did not go quite as far as Jean des Glaïeuls, settling in Capri.

The Adelswärd scandal did not break until the serialization of "Fleurs d'éther et de talus" was complete, but it did so in time to place a damper on further exercises in a similar vein. Fabrice did not abandon his chronicling of the seamier side of Parisian social life for some years, but he was a good deal more careful thereafter, and had moderated his tone considerably by the time the Great War put a final end to the Belle Époque in 1914. By then he had begun writing comedies for children based on the antique works of the Comtesse de Ségur, and the great majority of his publications after 1918 were action-adventure stories written for the juvenile market. It is not known whether he still exchanged letters with Liane de Pougy—who first became a princess by marriage, and then a nun, devoting her final years to piety and good works—but one suspects not. At any rate, "Fleurs d'éther et de talus" marked the effective end of a strange era in the career of "Delphi Fabrice" as well as a distinct phase of liberalism in the literary treatment of themes of homosexuality and drug use.

It cannot be claimed that "Fleurs d'éther et de talus" is a very good work; it suffers considerably from having been made up as the author went along, and the changes of name to which some of the characters are arbitrarily subjected are symptomatic of other inconsistencies in the author's planning, or lack of it. It never quite makes up its mind as to what kind of work it is and what it is trying to accomplish; its belated half-hearted attempt to pass itself off as a horror story in the same vein as *L'Araignée rouge* might well have been a response to editorial intrusion, always the bane of writers of feuilleton serials, ever-vulnerable to the pressure of reader reaction. In spite of its faults and hesitations, though—and to some extent because of them—it remains an interesting and intriguing text. It does not live up to its own perverse ambitions, but it would have been impossible for the author to follow through in those ambitions fully; he was, after all, working for a daily newspaper whose editors, although uncommonly liberal and ready to take risks by the standards of the day, had to maintain a certain level of diplomacy. It was always inevitable that Jean des Glaïeuls would be sent into the exile foretold in the first chapter of the text, but he did not die, even if he was eventually reduced to a diplomatic by-line, just as his ostensible and actual creators were.

There are worse fates, so it is said—but who am I to judge?

This translation was made from the relevant issues of the *Lanterne Supplement* reproduced on the Bibliothèque Nationale's *gallica* website, with the aid of its invaluable triple zoom function.

—Brian Stableford, August 2020.

FLOWERS
OF
ETHER

EYES OF FADED CORNFLOWER BLUE
(*Le Supplement*, 1 January 1903)

For Polaire[1]

A blue exists of which I die,
Because it is in your eyes!

"OH, you also know those lines by des Glaïeuls?" "Not 'his' lines but lines by Sully-Prudhomme, which that poor Jean loved to serve up to us."

"What are you saying, my dear? You know that he was my friend for long months."

"Yes, he was attributed to you as a lover. Fundamentally, I never believed it. Des Glaïeuls was

---

1 The cabaret artiste "Polaire" (Émélie-Marie Bouchard. 1874-1939) was scheduled to play the central part in Fabrice's play *L'Araignée rouge* in 1900 before the censor banned it. She went on to spectacular success, first on the stage, two years later, playing Claudine in the dramatization of Colette's novels (then credited to Willy) and then as a recording artist and star of silent movies.

21

so bizarre that I can willingly imagine that you paraded him for the gallery. Jean des Glaïeuls, produced by you at your suppers and in your dressing-room at the Folies-Bergère, his eternal shivering in his furs, with his white hands and their thirty-seven rings, all incite me to believe that you were amusing yourself a little by enriching your legend as a perverse woman."

"But my dear, 'friend' doesn't always mean 'lover.'"

"Tell me about it! But let's return to the subject. Why were you momentarily astonished, my little Fleur de Chiqué, to find me quoting to you:

A blue exists of which I die,
Because it is in your eyes!

"Two pretty lines, certainly . . . speak, I'm listening."

We were rolling, Nine d'Aubusson and I, through a blonde autumn night, all misty moonlight, along the Boulevard de Grenelle, where my whimsy so often led me to linger until pale dawn in quest of adventures—of all adventures, voluptuous, tragic or simply droll.

We had left the hired carriage at the corner of the boulevard and the Rue Croix-Nivert while we wandered at hazard. Nine, whose display of sham vices had earned her the nickname Fleur de Chiqué in the demi-monde where such names are given, had insisted on accompanying me. In her pretty head, curious for sensation, a night in Grenelle was a Walpurgisnacht populated by murders and amours, blood and kisses—only, all those horrors were narrated anecdotally, with gallant cut-throats who evidently returned belated ladies to their carriages after having crumpled their skirts, for form's sake.

At any rate, adventure was not flourishing at all, and two o'clock in the morning was approaching while we were still striding along the boulevard without finding anything that was not in the domain of utter banality. After having witnessed a sickening battery of drunkards, two or three disputes of whores and seigneurs—or *saigneurs*—with kiss-curls, all at a distance, from as far away as possible, we had decided to return to the carriage. It was then that, alluding to the faded cornflower blue eyes of a lady lingering in the halo of illumination of a street-lamp, I had murmured in my companion's ear the two lines so often repeated by Jean des Glaïeuls, a friend of feasting and ennui, who had departed abruptly two years before for the land of pearls and green poison.

One last glance at the boulevard . . .

In the black night, the hostile night, red eyes of gaslight were burning. The last tavern was closing. Our evening was definitely over. We were going home—or rather, I was taking Nine home.

She said: "Yes, those two lines cited by you just now amused me; and I can admit to you, my dear, that they caused a memory to resurface that is worth as much as all the curiosities you might have shown me tonight. It was a few years ago, in this quarter, behind the École Militaire, and as I've done with you tonight, that I escorted des Glaïeuls in his noctambulism. Des Glaïeuls! Is he not equally fond of the night and its emotions? Exactly as on the present occasion, we had run around the dance-halls, brasseries and other gallant houses, even hideous hooligan bars, fruitlessly, when one of us noticed two Arlequines run aground outside the carnival and the quarters of folly, behind a high brutal nickel counter. With shapely arms and slender waists, with figures as slim as one could wish, the two escapees from a costume ball were drinking alcohol and exchanging slightly spicy remarks with the barman. Their voices had soft inflexions, their extremities were rather fine and their laughter nervous, devoid of rascality . . .

"'Those are two ladies also in search of strong sensations,' said des Glaïeuls, smiling. 'Let's try to uncover their identity.' And he advanced gallantly, making contact

with voice and gesture

with the Arlequines, who, surprised and jibbing at first, relaxed as far as accepting snacks and cigarettes. They were truly attractive. Pretty faces could be divined beneath the masks that they refused to take off, and as soon as I had taken account of the fact that they both had eyes of the faded cornflower blue so beloved by des Glaïeuls, I understood my cavalier's enthusiasm. So at the exit from the tavern, I was not unduly surprised to see our friend quit me at the portière of my carriage and depart in a marauding fiacre for Maxim's, in the company of the two disguised individuals.

"It was at Maxim's, between six and seven o'clock the following day, that I obtained forceful commentaries on the news of des Glaïeuls 'good fortune.'

"'It's ignoble,' thundered some of the ladies, while a few others, more indulgent, countered with: 'It's quite amusing!'

"That poor des Glaïeuls, having disembarked in the Rue Royale and gone upstairs to a private cabinet with his two conquests, after the obligatory supper, persuaded his Arlequines—who had refused until then—finally to unmask. And as the couple hesitated, consulting one another with their gazes, with stifled laughter, he had abruptly and unexpectedly snatched away the two masks. What a tableau! The couple was mixed, a man and a woman; des Glaïeuls had abducted a couple of young lovers, who, after leaving a ball in the Latin quarter, had undertaken an excursion to the eccentric quarters. Des Glaïeuls face! Then annoyance, before the artstudentesque gibes of the young couple, the arrival of a maître d'hôtel and, finally, the divulgence of the adventure downstairs in the hall, where all the tables had laughed to tears. Meanwhile, Marcel Baron,[1] his hat tipped further over his ear than ever, had repeated at the top of his voice, brandishing his glass of champagne:

A blue exists of which I die,
Because it is in your eyes!

---

1 Marcel Baron (1872-1956) was a painter, nowadays classified as a "Modernist" by art-dealers in search of a convenient label.

"And that is one of the reasons that pushed that great madman Jean des Glaïeuls to depart for the land dear to Goncourt and Pierre Loti," concluded Nine d'Aubusson, "and it ought also to explain to you why these quarters, which are said to be so rich in sinister stories, can only remind me of amusing and mocking memories."

The carriage traversed the Pont de la Concorde and we re-entered the Paris of the boulevard . . .

A SESSION WITH WILD BEASTS
(*Le Supplement*, 17 January 1903)

For Liane de Lancy[1]

"WE can't part like this," I said to Nine d'Aubusson, huddled in her furs in the depths of the coupé. "Here we are in the Place de la Concorde, which is to say, at Maxim's; our excursion through nocturnal Grenelle must have given you a little appetite; let's go and refresh ourselves a little."

"On one condition—or, rather, on two conditions."

"What are they?"

"We don't go to Maxim's, where, at this hour— two o'clock in the morning—there are too many *dames and messieurs de l'amour et du hazard*, singing,

---

1 "Liane de Lancy" was the pseudonym of one of the "professional beauties" of *fin-de-siècle* Paris society, thus labeled in a famous painting by Henri de Toulouse-Lautrec, which depicts her skating in the Palais de Glace in the Champs-Élysées, in the company of Édouard Dujardin. She was also painted by Jacques-Henri Lartigue at Auteuil racecourse, with the similarly pseudonymous Berthe Fontana.

and above all drinking . . . and you know that I detest drunkards . . ."

"Granted . . . but the other condition, if you please?"

"Will you be having supper too?"

"That, of course, never. It's a bad habit that I had too much difficulty breaking to take it up again. Anyway, you know that I have the worst stomach in Paris."

"Well, confess that you haven't stolen it. One doesn't devote oneself for years to ether and hashish with impunity. But that isn't the question . . ."

And Nine, that dear Flower of Affectation, became more pressing. In the shadow, her gold-flecked eyes were strangely insistent. "Come on, my dear Fabrice, sup with me—something trivial, if you wish, but sup!"

I finally accepted, and threw out the address of the Café de Paris. The coupé, already in the Rue Royale, where lines of carriages were snaking to infinity, headed for the Avenue de l'Opéra via the boulevards, and Nine and I resumed our conversation amid the noise of little bells, so monotonous and calming.

Now she cited to me a few of the celebrated follies of our friend Jean des Glaïeuls—follies that were quite typical of the tastes and mores of that young man, who, with all the seriousness in the world, received guests at his table in a pink silk jacket, green waistcoat and lace ruff, in a dining room of the purest Renaissance, from the furniture to the silverware and even the festooned tablecloth authentically originating from Saint-Megrin, the darling of the handsome

Henri—a provenance nothing less than proven.[1] Then she talked to me about the study-dressing-room of that tormented spirit, the Louis XV desk next to the dressing-table and the secretaire next to the looking-glass, the pink marble dressing-table laden with perfumes and make-up, neighboring flasks and boxes with large spiders naturalized in museum display-cases. A true madman, what!"

"All right," I said to Nine, interrupting her in flight, "let's not enumerate the follies of des Glaïeuls. It would take us too far!"

On that, we both had an equivocal smile. And I continued: "But you don't know his most amusing adventure—that of the handsome lion-tamer . . . ? Exactly: the handsome lion-tamer."

"The lion-tamer Darck?"

"I admire your penetration."

"Is that a joke?"

"Oh, my dear, you're exaggerating my merits and yours. But if you begin by being witty we'll no longer understand one another."

And to cut short that flirtation I told the beautiful child the story of the lion-tamer Darck and des Glaïeuls.

"The tamer Darck! All Paris—what am I saying? All France, and even Belgium—has seen him, and he's

1 "Saint-Mégrin" was the name of a young sixteenth-century nobleman said to have been killed by Henri de Lorrain, Duc de Guise, for sleeping with his wife, Catherine de Nevers—at least, that is the way that Alexandre Dumas' play based on the story tells it; Fabrice seems to be suggesting a different interpretation.

as popular in Montmartre as in Nantes, on the Quai de la Fosse or in Old Marseille. Eternally costumed in deerskin, squeezed into yellow velvet waistcoats that emphasize his wasp waist, with Russian leather boots, he parades his feline moustache everywhere, with his airs of a fortunate man, and his wild beasts, especially his terrible lion Dominator.

"And it's that man, known for having ruined several demi-mondaines, that Jean des Glaïeuls had attached to his chariot. They were always seen, and always together, at the wrestling-matches at the Folies Bergère, in the wings of the Olympia and around the dressing-room of Louise Willy,[1] the famous mime, whose crystalline laugh des Glaïeuls loves so much—them and always them, late into the night, at the high counters of the American Bar in the Madeleine quarter, Darck always exhibiting his manner of a man excessively beloved, des Glaïeuls more sprightly and dressed up than ever, his cravats sensationally gaudy and his hands more ring-laden than ever. You can imagine how commentaries on that couple ran riot, can't you, my dear? But what an explosion there was when the rumor spread along the boulevards and through the music halls of the forthcoming fairground debut of Jean des Glaïeuls. The poor lunatic had thought it droll to exhibit himself in the middle of the fair of Grenelle in Darck's menagerie surround-

1 "Louise Willy," to whom Fabrice dedicated a subsequent item in the present series, was one of the first cabaret artistes whose act was filmed (hence the reference to her celebrity as a "mime") and remains famous for being filmed performing a strip-tease in 1896.

ed by lions and lionesses held in respect by the tamer; he planned to dance Louis XV motifs. The laurels of Madame Bob Walter[1] and other Julianos did not prevent him from sleeping.

"So, that evening, at Grenelle, the menagerie was taken by storm. The entire boulevard was there, represented by its women and men of joy and prey, crowded around the central cage—a central cage decked with buttercup-yellow and Nile-green scarves, and flowering with gladioli—noblesse oblige!—brought from Nice at great expense. To depict the impatience of all those people avid for scandal would be impossible for me. They got ready to whistle in the clan of cigars, while in the band of fans, on the contrary, they opted for unfavorable murmurs, women having more indulgence for the vagaries of the heart.

"Finally, the session commenced. At first there were the insignificant exercises of a gladiator with the muzzle of a jackal, succeeded by that of a woman seventy years old at the least, whose painted face was reminiscent of a crepe. Then an aide announced des Glaïeuls' dances,

---

1 "Bob Walter" (Baptistine Dupré, 1856-1907) was an exotic dancer who became internationally famous in the 1890s; her specialty was performing a version of Loïe Fuller's famous "serpentine dance" in a cage with four lions held at bay by a tamer named Marck, which she repeated many times between 1894 and 1899; Jean Lorrain was remarkably hostile in his critiques of her performance and she once assaulted him publicly at the première of one of his plays—an incident recapitulated in Jane de La Vaudère's *Les Androgynes*. The subsidiary reference to "other Julianos" is presumably to the prolific composer of dance music who often signed himself A. P. Juliano (Auguste Pilate or Pilati, 1810-1877).

to a general 'Aha!' Almost immediately, the young man appeared, more Louis XV than ever in his silks and lace, preceded by Darck, who, pitchfork in hand, got ready to hold the beasts in respect.

"Scarcely had the Adonis sketched his first steps, however, the lions not having been introduced as yet, when a woman burst into the arena, bustling the stupefied employees aside. Before the central cage, she launched at Jean des Glaiüels a resounding: 'Filthy swine!' and then at Darck, who had suddenly gone green: 'Disgusting individual! It's for this dung-heap that you desert your wife and children!' And Madame Darck—for it was her—before the public from whom the tamer had been draining kisses and money for so many years, howled, along with insults, her sad story, unknown to everyone, like her very existence: her life of privations and poverty in the depths of Clichy, near the river bank, where her husband had dumped her with three kids!

"From green, Darck went red, and then white, like a chameleon. Under the lash of the final insult, he ran away, under the jeers of the crowd, followed by Jean des Glaïeuls, who was kneading and tearing his lace handkerchief, and who made his exit ashamedly, walking backwards. As Jane de Nancy said on quitting the menagerie: 'Jean de Glaïeuls didn't come back. That changed him!'

"You can imagine that the scandal was the talk of Paris! People were gossiping about it for a fortnight . . .

"But we've arrived, my dear Nine, and since you're hungry . . ."

The carriage stopped outside the Café de Paris.

HER ADVERTISEMENT!
(*Le Supplement*, 24 January 1903)

For Jane de Lancy[1]

AT a small table in the Café de Paris, Nine d'Aubusson and I were nibbling a supper, both fatigued by music and heady perfumes—and yet the gypsies were executing the catchiest marches of Ganne and the most energetic waltzes of Goublier.[2] Exhausted by an excursion to Grenelle, however, without having been able to collect any unfamiliar sensation there, and stunned by the return journey in the tintinnabulating carriage and the mutual confidences exchanged by half-closed eyes and immobile fur-clad bodies, we

---

1 Possibly a misprint, accidentally combining the previously-cited names of Jane de Nancy and Liane de Lancy; the name Jane de Lancry also crops up occasionally in lists of names in the *Supplement*'s gossip column, in items probably supplied by Fabrice; the "professional beauties" of Paris tended to be a trifle imitative in their choice of pseudonyms.
2 The references are to the composers Louis-Gaston Ganne (1862-1923) and "Gustave Goublier" (Gustave Conin, 1856-1926).

were scarcely in a state to shine. And certainly, it had required a stupid self-esteem of appearing still and always Parisian, in the latest style, for us to run aground at half past three in the morning in that nocturnal café, amid the crowd of partygoers, where black suits cast a somber note into the professional elegance of all those ladies-for-hire.

Truly, we were asleep on our feet, neither of us daring to admit it to the other, and yet devoid of strength. Perhaps I was about to risk talking about leaving when a couple insinuated themselves between the tables and came to take their place facing us, a couple whose entrance on stage required our attention.

The woman was small and round, giving the impression of three superimposed lemons, a small one for the head, a medium-sized one for the upper body and a large one for the rest, with tenebrous eyes that squinted in a face the hue of old ivory, framed by tresses so black they were blue; she was exhibiting large jewels of charcuterie at the end of singularly short arms. She imposed the idea of a hilarious frog, above all at the moments when she aimed her lorgnon, whose mount then had golden reflections.

The man, a handsome enough fellow, well-built, with brown hair worn rather long, a fascinating gaze and flamboyant gestures, offered, with his fat face and the satisfied smile that flowered on his mouth, the type of a freedman of the low Empire. With the guttural voice of a child of the faubourgs he ordered a supper from the hasty maître-d'hôtel.

"Good," said Nine, leaning toward me. "When one mentions the wolf . . . do you recognize him?"

"Of course, the tamer Drack,[1] the scandalous tamer Drack, dear from all points of view to the alcoves of the demi-monde, the handsome tamer one of whose adventures I related to you a little while ago. I thought, however, that he had fallen to the extent of not being able to get up again . . . his menagerie seized and sold; his best lion, Dominator, dead; a shady bankruptcy, and frauds that nearly brought their author before the judges of the new chambre . . . I repeat that I thought him sunk forever . . . but who's that he's with?"

"Laure Javel, known as the Three-Lemon Kid or the National Squint. You know, the Javel who obtained such a fine flop by exhibiting a clever goose on the stage of the Folies Bergère.

> But the silliest of the geese
> Wasn't the one you might think!

as I know not what amorphous poet rhymed. Come on, don't you recognize her?"

"That's true," I replied. "I know Mademoiselle Laure Javel, and I even had the pleasure, a few months ago, at receiving from that demoiselle, at Maxim's, a rather . . . *engueulatoire* letter.[2] It appears that she was

---

1 The change in the tamer's name might also be a consequence of the typesetter being unable to read Fabrice's handwriting, although he might have decided that the original version echoed the name of Bob Walter's associate too closely.

2 The word *engueulatoire* enjoyed a brief vogue after being invented by the cabaret artiste Aristide Bruant in one of his comic songs. It implies that the letter was coarsely insulting. Fabrice did not get along well with Bob Walter's successors in

moved by a scribbled article. But tell me, my dear Nine, La Javel must have a great deal of money, to have hitched up Drack? I know the fellow; he's expensive . . . and then, to replace a tamer at the head of a menagerie costs a lot more than putting a suburban tenor in her furniture!"

"Has La Javel got money? But my dear, no more than anyone else, no more than me. She has her nice little house and its habitués, three titled lovers, one of whom is a Brazilian, the same one who gave her the house in the Rue de Prony, where everyone is received with open curtains."

"Oh, dear friend, that's almost unworthy of you. And then, he's been punished so harshly!"

"Almost as much as the demoiselle to which I've applied it, no? So, I was saying that the Three-Lemon Kid isn't, at present, more fortunate than the rest of us. When I say 'us' I'm forgetting that I have the most beautiful pearls in Paris.[1] But she has one thing more than the majority of these ladies; she's intelligent. Perfectly: in-tell-i-gent! She knows how to handle her advertising. It's her advertisement that's in the process of making her one of the foremost demi-mondaines in Paris . . ."

"And that advertisement?"

Marck's act; one of them successfully sued him for defamation after an uncomplimentary review some while after this story was published, perhaps having construed the description of Laure Javel as a caricature of her.

1 Liane de Pougy boasted of having the most beautiful pearls in Paris—perhaps a little too loudly, as they were stolen in a burglary that became a major news story in the spring of 1903.

"Is Drack himself."

"Don't understand."

"You will."

And Nine, becoming a little animated, continued:

"I repeat to you: she's intelligent. And the fashion in which she has operated, and is operating again with Drack, is proof of the intelligence that I grant her, and which your half-smile seems to be denying. Look, a moment ago, you were astonished that a demi-elegant woman like her has enough money to hold on to the handsome tamer. Do you know her method of procedure, the means imagined by her? It's quite simple, and the story has been running around the Palais de Glace for eighteen months—the eighteen months that the couple has already squandered in amorous games!"

And Nine d'Aubusson, completely awakened by the idea of extracting a little story from her bag, dipped her lips in her glass of Roederer and, with her elbows on the table, and her joined hands sustaining her chin, she went on:

"When Laure Javel found Drack, he was on his uppers, abandoned by everyone, his menagerie sold and his last hopes flown away. So great was his distress that he had even set aside his pride and gone to work for Edmond Pezon, his rival of the previous day.[1] But the

---

1 Edmond Pezon (1868-1916), a member of a famous family of lion-tamers, distinguished himself from his father, uncles, siblings and cousins when he was badly mauled by a lioness in 1889. A series of adventure stories published under Pezon's name as his "memoirs" is credited in some bibliographies as having been ghost-written by Fabrice and Oscar Méténier.

fellow, like the player he still is, had not abandoned all hope of a return to fortune. He awaited patiently the lady whom his biceps would arouse and his boldness before the wild beasts would render amorous—and it was Laure Javel, troubled by champagne, light and noise one evening at the Neuilly fair, who suddenly became infatuated with the tamer. As bold as a page, she abducted him in mid-session and did him the honors of the little house in the Rue Prony that same evening. The next day, either out of brazenness or amorous gratitude, she paid off Drack's debt to Pezon, dressed her tamer and exhibited him to the little friends at Armenonville. The Three-Lemon Kid's infatuation was the talk of partying society; the *Supplement* consecrated an item to it in its gossip column, and two other newspapers followed suit, and an American railway or pork king sought an introduction to the amorous lady . . .

"In brief, that little escapade, cleverly exploited by Laure, was worth a redoubling of her glory and prosperity. Immediately, the demoiselle consecrated thousands to reestablishing Drack's affairs. She wrote to the merchants of wild beasts in Hamburg, bought lions, and fitted out a caravan, the modern-style Menagerie Drack! But of course, warned of the fashion in which the handsome tamer discarded his lovers, she put everything in her name: carriages, cages and animals . . ."

Nine paused for two seconds, drank, and then continued:

"And that situation has lasted for eighteen months, eighteen months during which Laure Javel, who is certainly not beautiful, has been offering herself sensuality while increasing her income. For that is the miracle, a very Parisian miracle: her liaison with Drack gives her a nimbus of glory, creating in her regard, among foreigners, an unhealthy but productive curiosity. The Three-Lemon Kid takes account of that and exploits it, cultivating her amorous legend as a man-tamer with a consummate art. Her kept man has become her advertisement. Don't you find that supremely skillful?"

Nine d'Aubusson uttered a pretty laugh, which uncovered the rice-grains of her teeth, and then said: "Pass me the cumin; you know how fond I am of that spice . . ."

THE MAN OF PREY
(*Le Supplement*, 31 January 1903)

For Mary de Livrof[1]

"DECIDEDLY," I said to Nine, "that tamer Drack is a very sad individual; entertained by women and by men, he's complete! And to think that all his scandalous stories don't place him beyond the pale of public opinion!"

"Entirely the contrary," my friend replied. "It poses the pretty fellow. Anyway, see for yourself. The little Duc d'Arles has approached his table and is chatting to him. And here comes Prince Nevrinski too . . . and also Marcel Marchand, the friend of grand dukes . . ."

In fact, that trio of Parisians was standing before the table occupied by Laure Javel, a.k.a. the Three-Lemon Kid and her lover of the heart. The latter, his gestures broad and his voice loud, was giving explanations on the subject of an accident that had

---

1 The blonde "Mary de Livrof" crops up regularly in the *Supplement*'s gossip column, in lists of names of women seen at social events in 1905-06, but mentions of her are rare elsewhere.

happened to him a few days earlier in the course of a performance in his Modern-Style Menagerie. And how Drack dramatized the thing; what a bloody tale he extracted from a simple scratch!

"It's quite simple," he repeated to the three clubmen—and, in reality, to the entire gallery—"I came into the cage for the second session of the evening and they sent me Sultan. Scarcely has he entered than he growls, shows his teeth and glares at me in a fashion to which I wasn't accustomed. Immediately, I have a presentiment, and I say to myself: 'Drack, you're done for!' But, courageous, as I always am, I don't hesitate, and although I don't have a pitchfork I advance toward Sultan. Then he bounds, grabs hold of me, digs his claws into the meat . . . I fall to my knees . . . without abandoning my sang-froid I seize my revolver, fire three shots—blanks, of course—into the animal's mouth . . . Stunned, his muzzle roasted, he recoils . . . I free myself, get up, and exit amid a thunder of applause. All the same, I was really hurt . . ."

And the three men of the world expanded themselves in admiring remarks on the tamer's courage— old Nevrinski especially, doubtless no longer remembering his lineage of Polish heroes. It was sickening— enough to make one vomit, I tell you.

"He's got them eating out of his hand, hasn't he?" murmured Nine d'Aubusson. "The entire Café de Paris is besotted with that tamer; can't you feel it? And are you taking account of the consideration that is rebounding on Laure Javel, the tamer's tamer! Look at the desirous eyes of the women for Drack and of the men for the Three-Lemon Kid. Do you believe now in the intelligence of that cunning woman?"

"But in sum, how is it," I hazarded, "that the handsome lion-tamer, conscious of his prestige and feminine homages, doesn't let go of the cross-eyed Laure, who, as you've told me yourself, has put the menagerie in her own name—which is to say, leaving Drack in a humiliating inferiority. I'm astonished that that man of prey doesn't leave the Three-Lemon Kid and the Modern-Style Menagerie in order to have himself offered a new caravan in his own name by one of those ladies of amour and hazard . . . opportunities can't be lacking."

"Come on, my dear Fabrice," Nine replied. "When you've reflected that an installation like the Modern-Style Menagerie represents fifty thousand francs, at least, you'll admit that, in these times of bad business, demoiselles susceptible of offering handouts of that magnitude aren't found on every street corner . . . or anywhere else. Drack knows that full well. That's why he holds to the Laure Javel plan, privately convinced that one day he'll 'have' the National Squint just as he 'had' poor Deverny . . . you remember Deverny?"

"Of course I remember Deverny," I said. "I even knew her! Old Deverny, maintained, and on a re-spectable footing, by Champolbert, the champagne merchant; old Deverny, long and dry, with a big head surmounted by hair horribly tinted red. looking like a milliner's mushroom. Deverny! Were there enough jokes about her sexless person, reminiscent of a mama-mouchi and a fortune-teller, her waxy shoulders and her pelican gait! And her pretention to command, everyone and everywhere, the sovereign attitude of that mummified grotesque, which made her seem a hundred years old—at least—and earned her the nickname of the Queen of the Ruins! Yes, I remember Deverny, but I repeat, my dear, that I knew her."

"Well then, you must recall her disaster."

"Perfectly. You've put me on the track. Her disaster was one of Drack's coups—the first."

With that, Nine and I both evoked that sentimental and financial story, a contemporary chapter of "How amour returns to old men . . . or women," if I might put it thus. What a cruel story, and how Parisian—what am I saying?—how human!

"It happened six years ago. Drack was then twenty-four, and felt as free as a fish in water—which he was, for, although he had committed the folly of marrying before leaving for his military service, he had relegated his wife and three kids to a hole in the suburbs. Initially a petty actor on the stages of the faubourgs, he had quickly understood that for an illiterate, the stage cannot lead to anything much. At the most, he could hope to become illustrious in café-concerts, but there, in view of the competition, the future was uncertain. So, one day, he thought, bravely, of becoming a lion tamer. The métier was undoubtedly dangerous, but the handsome fellow said to himself *Bah! Let's risk the packet. I'm no windier than the next man. We'll see.* He introduced himself to old Père Rezon,[1] soon having the fellow in hand.

"Three months later, he made his debut at the Neuilly fair, that gala of fairground folk, and from the first evening, carried away the public . . . and the heart of Deverny, the old and proud Deverny, who had come into the Rezon menagerie, to her misfortune. What a thunderbolt! La Deverny took the tamer away after the performance, as so many women were later to do, including Laure Javel.

"Oh, that first night of amour in a wretched hotel in Levallois-Perret—the old fay hadn't dared to take her prey home, because of the domestics—inhabited by Limousins who made a lot of noise going to work at dawn, just at the hour when the exhausted Queen of the Ruins was going to sleep, her ears ringing and her body dead in Drack's arms!

"That night determined the entire lives of those two individuals; La Deverny threw out the old man who was maintaining her and installed as master in her house in the Boulevard Pereire the young man of prey, whose savant caresses had bewitched her forever, Drack cultivated the lust of his keeper in order to conquer her, and on the day that he thought his empire firmly established over the cardboard Elisabeth, he asked her boldly for a menagerie. Three months later, the first Drack menagerie was founded, and La Deverny, having sold her house, established herself

---

1 Perhaps a misprint for Pezon induced by misread handwriting, but probably a substitution, Fabrice having become more careful in the employment of real names in his fiction.

in the caravan with her lover. The latter, initially grateful for the old woman's sacrifices, then began to find her tedious. Soon, drunk on success and women, the Queen of the Ruins became odious to him, all the more so because, as jealous as a tigress, she made scenes over everything and nothing—scenes after which she offered him rings, cravat-pins, etc. in order to be forgiven. Two years after setting up a household with the tamer, she was ruined, cleaned out to the last franc, so laboriously acquired in thirty years of prostitution, Drack having devoured seven thousand francs, almost to the sou, set aside by that ant who, professionally, had played the grasshopper for thirty years . . .

"Then, the ponce revealed himself entirely. One evening, after a violent argument, he beat La Deverny up and threw her out. The unfortunate woman wept, begged, and then threatened. Drack, inflexible, departed for foreign parts with his menagerie and stayed away for two years, gambling, partying and running around with women. It was then that his first fall occurred . . .

"Well," I said to Nine, "the same fate awaits Laure Javel. It might be more or less distant, but it will come. One doesn't play with fire with impunity."

"And Deverny?" my friend asked. "Do you know what became of her?"

"I'm told that she consoled herself in absinthe . . ."

"Pooh!"

". . . and that, in order to live, she sells fritters at the Porte de Billancourt."

THE AMOROUS WOMAN
OF THE RIVER-BANK
(*Le Supplement*, 7 February 1903)

For Louise Willy

"BILLANCOURT! You're evoking Billancourt," said Nine d'Aubusson, suddenly. "Oh, how many things that name, dropped by you, recalls to my memory!"

"Tell me about it?"

"Yes, in order for you to serve my little stories to your readers! Thank you! Come back tomorrow!"

"But I assure you, my dear Nine . . ."

"Don't assure me of anything. I have no confidence in you, my dear Fabrice. That's not my fault . . . am I making myself clear?"

Nine d'Aubusson uttered a little nervous laugh, and then got up. "Let's go!" she commanded. "It's after four o'clock in the morning. It's time to go to bed. Anyway, observe that here in the Café de Paris, the spectacle is beginning to lack interest. Laure Javel is leaving with Drack, her handsome tamer; Liane d'Artagnan is sketching her habitual scene to Carmosine, her excessively intimate girl-friend; Edwige de Nancy is serving up her macabre pseudo-amours to Prince Nevrinski, who is definitely getting increasingly senile,[1] and Marcel Marchand has just raised his voice by an octave. It's time; let's go!"

And we left. Outside, there was still the mildness of that blond autumn night, a night of languishment and dream; the Avenue de l'Opéra was asleep, all the windows closed, behind its dead stones.

"Oh, if you weren't fatigued . . . !" I murmured to Nine.

"Well?"

"Well, instead of each going to our homes, we could go, like virtuous people, to take a cup of milk at the Tour de Villebon."

"You're mad! But your folly pleases me. So be it. Let's go. I'll get up at six o'clock in the evening . . ."

"Me, at seven, as usual . . ."

"And although, a little while ago, when we arrived at the Café de Paris, I was literally exhausted because of our noctambulism in Grenelle. I've now recovered my strength, and I'm fresh and fit; let's go to Villebon. We'll leave the carriage in Meudon and we'll go up to the tower, *on our claws*, as our friend Méténier says . . . yes, leaning on one another like two 'little blue flowers' of the Rue de la Paix. It will be idyllic, ridiculous and charming!"

---

1 The story of Edwige de Nancy's macabre reputation is told in *L'Araignée rouge*.

With that, Nine d'Aubusson laughed again, and, after having ordered the surly and ill-assured coachman to make his way slowly to Meudon via the quays—all the quays, from the Place de la Concorde to the Pont de Saint-Cloud—we plunged into the coupé.

"You're not forgetting, my dear, that we're going to pass through Billancourt?" I insinuated to my friend. "Billancourt, the name of which, pronounced before you, refreshed your memory, you admitted to me just now . . . well, be generous, and tell me your stories of Billancourt. In any case, are we not both near to confessions . . . and since yesterday evening, have we not been exchanging gossip? What do a few items more or less matter? It costs you so little, and it gives me so much pleasure. I'm listening . . ."

"That Fabrice!" sighed Nine, lighting a cigarette of blond tobacco.[1] "You do whatever you want with me. So I'm going to tell you about my adventure in Billancourt—or, rather, my double adventure, for it has two compartments, like all respectable adventures. But you'll promise me never to write it?"

"That's promised."

"Good."

She settled into a corner of the carriage, with a rustle of silk, and in a slightly veiled voice, between two puffs of Richmond, confessed in her turn, in phrases half-sincere and half-literary, in which I saluted in

1 The gossip column of the *Supplement* included references in 1903 to Liane de Pougy's habit of chain-smoking rolled-up cigarettes of "blond tobacco."

passing, like old acquaintances, Bourget, Zola and even phrases of my own:

"Just now, when we were coming back from Grenelle, I recounted an adventure of Jean des Glaïeuls, that friend whom the world gives me as a lover, and I concluded by declaring to you that the eccentric quarters, which are believed to be so laden with sinister stories, could only remind me of amusing and mocking memories. Well, I was wrong, because Billancourt gave me the most intense impression of anguish that it is possible to experience—and don't mock. I'm not, at this moment, Mademoiselle Fleur de Chiqué . . .

"I was six months ago in the month of November. I was passing through Paris, having returned from Berlin, where I had just been playing in a pantomime, and was about to leave for Cairo, to which another engagement summoned me. The little Duc d'Arles, of course, my lord and master, composed a vigilant guard of honor for me—so vigilant that on getting off the train at the Gare de l'Est I had pretexted an irresistible need to go and embrace my mother, in order to plant that excessively adhesive lover there, at least for a few days.

"Prayers, threats and various scenes on the part of the sire—nothing had been able to stop me, and, in the final count, before my obstinacy, the little duc had given me permission to go and spend a week *en famille* with my mother, in the middle of Boulogne-sur-Seine, that land of laundresses.

"Ah, Boulogne—that's my native land; it's there, as a little girl, that I played hopscotch, and, a little later, allowed my first pair of silk garters to be attached by a boy, for—and I'm confiding this to you alone—my first gift of amour was a pair of silk garters worth a good nineteen sous!

"Soon, I was next to Maman, who still lives in the little dwelling where I was born. Amazed and joyful to see myself installed with her, I reconquered, along with my little girl's bed, all the pretty blue dreams of my childhood: those lovely dreams that remained nested for so long in the creases of the cretonne curtains. I forgot—with what delight!—the petty actress that I am, Parisian life, racecourses, Maxim's and the Palais de Glace; I forgot everything, my house, my horses and my lover, in order to play the little housewife. A very simple tailored dress, a fox-fur around my neck and a felt boater on my head, with a minuscule basket over my arm, I slipped into the streets of Boulogne early in the morning, going to buy provisions, to the great alarm of the neighbors, who could not believe their eyes on seeing a famous actress—for in Boulogne I pass for a famous actress—going into the baker's to buy a pound-and-a-half loaf of bread. Their stupor stimulated my joy. I felt like Marie-Antoinette playing farmer's wife in the Petit Trianon.

"The afternoons I spent on the waterside.

"Oh, that waterside! It's there that I truly rediscovered myself entirely, on the quay, between the guinguettes displaying their signs and the gray water balancing the boats and the pontoons. There, all my

childhood assailed me, rising to my brain as an intoxication and moistening my eyes. That waterside!
I saw myself again as a little girl in all the little girls I
encountered, all the little girls who, like me at the age
of ten, were teasing the boys and darting sly gazes at
them in which poorly-formulated desires were already
legible. Oh, that waterside! What a perfume, lenitive
and irritating at the same time, it exhaled for me! At a
certain moment, it was like a fire lit in my veins, and
I would have thrown myself upon the breast of the
first monsieur who had looked at me with desirous
eyes . . .

"Then I made a sign to Théophile, *Thophile*, a
handsome lad with soft eyes, with whom I had played
as a child; Thophile, who, attentive to my slightest
gestures, detached his boat. And we set forth on the
water, behind the Île de Billancourt, in the little arm
of the Seine, always deserted, full of rushes and nenu-
phars, and where, although so close to Paris, life seems
dead, torpid in the shade of tall trees agitated by a
perpetual frisson . . .

"You can guess what happened, can't you? But
confess that I had rights to happiness.

"One does not live with impunity for months on
end in an entourage of boors who only keep you and
exhibit you out of pride, the pride of a man brutalized
by partying, who parades a beautiful mistress as he
shows off a fine horse!

"Yes, with Thophile I let myself go, playing the
'little blue flower'; I had the soul of a milliner. Feeling
myself in his pithy arms, small and soft, losing my

hand in his—a hand so large that it seemed monstrous; a hand with a strong grip, as you, the man of the *Araignée rouge*, love them—I savored joyful minutes of passive sensuality; the sensuality of abandonment, so dear, so soft, so exquisite . . .

"I was his thing and his possession; I submitted to his caresses, I felt his breath upon me, his body swooning in my relaxed arms, then tightened, and then relaxed again, like the wings of a thrush fluttering through ripe vines . . .

"Jean des Glaïeuls would have given a lot to be in my place eh?"

Nine d'Aubusson interrupted herself in order to light another cigarette.

THE LADY OF THE OPALS
(*Le Supplement*, 14 February 1903)

For Angèle Delinière[1]

A ND Nine d'Aubusson continued:
    "My week of amour on the waterside with my
Thophile, a week of abandonment and spasms, a week
of forgetfulness and happiness . . . oh, it will sing for a
long time in my memory, that week! How good it was
to faint in *his* arms in that landscape . . ."

At that point I interrupted her, for I foresaw a
dangerous tirade.

"Yes, my dear Nine. I can see you coming. You're
about to bring out for me all the poorly-digested cli-
chés of your bad reading—you can see that I too am
being frank! You're going to lay out a petty landscape
for me that I and we, Huysmans and all his pupils,
have painted twenty times over: the landscapes of the

---

1 The name Delinière crops up in the *Supplement* in 1901 in
numerous lists of performers appearing at the Scala theater,
immediately after Polaire's name; the forename is added in a
review of the revue in question.

water and the sky at dusk, from the thin and imprecise horizon to the bank, the limp verticals of factory chimneys and the dark mass of the trees of the Île de Billancourt; and the water above all, the water like nacre and ash.

"Or you're going to offer me the tableau of the sunset, the sky lightly tinted with ink, the mirror of the water having still retained a little daylight in its silvering, an indecisive clarity that only releases regret. Yes, the water again, and always the water, the great defective ribbon of the river, corroded by darkness in the shadow of bridges and banks, the bridges whose aprons stripe the gray décor with a brutal streak of Indian ink . . .

"And then there will be further enthusiastic phrases on amour and its pleasures, the sweetness of loving as the days and the water go by, the entire display of a swooning in the arms of the male or the female—that depends on what sex one wants to have today . . . Excuse that outburst; it's the troubling memory of our friend Jean des Glaïeuls that's the cause of it . . . Jean des Glaïeuls of the as-yet-uncertain sex!

"Listen my dear Nine, and don't depict that literary landscape for me. My pockets are full of them; I sell them . . . so, rather tell me, briefly and without murmuring, about your adventure in Billancourt . . ."

"But I've only been doing that for half an hour!" Nine exclaimed, without getting annoyed at my outburst. "Only, truly, you're cutting off my effects!"

"You know full well that they don't work on me. I hate artificial means, and I'm for good and robust nature . . ."

"Yes," my friend interrupted, smiling, not without malice, "one is aware of your love of robustness . . . it's your turn not to make a show of yourself."

And with that, glad to have "stuck" me—at least, she thought she had—Nine d'Aubusson lit a third cigarette and continued her little confession.

"After my week of amorous and familial life, I quit Boulogne and my lover in order to rejoin the little Duc d'Arles, my lover, to go to Cairo. But in the meantime, the direction of the Théâtre Métropolitain out there had had the bad luck, which wasn't unusual, of going bankrupt, and I found myself in Paris in the middle of the theater season, without an engagement.

"Oh, you can't suspect the irritation that corrodes artistes without an engagement, the emptiness of their days and their bleak evenings: the Bois, the racecourses, the night cafés, the ordinary life of idlers, becomes their life, in sum.

"It was at that moment that Jean des Glaïeuls, who had just had a grand ballet, *Messaline s'ennuie*, accepted by the director of the Olympe-Plastique, hearing of my inaction, came to see me and proposed that I play a role in his piece. And what a role: Messaline herself! Messaline, the empress of lust, who had haunted the slumber of my nights for so many years; the royal whore, the illustrious prostitute.

"As you can imagine, I accepted. The day after the proposal, Jean des Glaïeuls introduced me to the director of the Olympe-Plastique, that poor Henri Commerce whose frantic passion for Marga de Violetta has led you know where . . . And I was accepted. That same evening, the whole Boulevard knew about my engagement; the next day all of France, and even foreign lands, had heard the news, thanks to one of those press communiqués, which only Henri Commerce's secretary, the intrepid Bois-sans-Soif, another who has disappeared, possessed the secret at that time.

"You can imagine how happy I was. Oh, yes, *there are things that a woman doesn't forget,* as a popular song has it. My amorous suffering left by the pleasant romance lived with Thophile, the suffering exacerbated by the rupture of my engagement in Cairo, disappeared. I was metamorphosed from one day to the next. I gave myself entirely to my role, and, I confess, Thophile dropped out of my memory.

> *Often, various woman*
> *Is as fickle as she is mad!*

Besides which, the rehearsals absorbed me too much. I arrived at the Olympe-Plastique at one o'clock in the afternoon, only to emerge at half past six in the evening, exhausted, done in, with my head on fire. I dined swiftly on two boiled eggs and a slice of smoked salmon and immediately afterwards I ran to Jean des Glaïeuls' house in the Rue Desbordes-Valmore, out there at the far end of Passy, to do more work, and to work seriously, for with Jean des Glaïeuls a woman doesn't waste her time in . . . bagatelles, does she? At two o'clock in the morning, no longer able to stand up, literally worn out, I slid into my bed, where the little Duc d'Arles no longer kept me any but fraternal company—oh, simply fraternal!

"Oh, my life in those two months, the formidable effort that I had to make in order to arrive at the height of the role confided to me, the multiple—so multiple!—rehearsals, my discouragements, my furies, my tantrums . . . and what tantrums! Jean des Glaïeuls retained the memory for a long time, for one evening, at his house, I let myself go to the extent of breaking more than a hundred louis' worth of rare ceramics, an entire collection of stoneware spiders signed Carriès, Lachenal and Dalpyrat.[1] It's true that the next day, ashamed of that fit of nerves, I sent in compensation to that demoiselle—or, rather, that monsieur—my portrait, enriched with diamonds . . .

All the same, although the role was admirable, I didn't take long to put an end to that life of a galley-slave—and you can guess whether that also saw the little Duc d'Arles condemned to a forced sagacity . . . at least in my company, for, in addition to me . . .

"The last rehearsals were a little before Christmas, and the premiere was announced with great noise, indiscretions in the press, fliers on all the walls, posters by Pal and even Cappiello, who was making his debut,[2] front pages in the major papers, illustrations signed Willette, Forain and Toulouse-Lautrec.[3] Jean

---

1 Jean-Joseph Carriès (1858-1894) became famous as a ceramist for his production of "horror masks"; Edmond Lachenal (1855-1948) and Pierre-Adrien Dalpayrat (1844-1910) were major figures in the development of art nouveau ceramics.
2 The references are to Jean de Paleolgu, or Paleologue (1855-1942), who often signed his posters "Pal," and Leonetto Cappiello (1875-1942).
3 Adolphe Willette (1857-1926) was a prolific illustrator and caricaturist who also painted walls and ceilings in numerous

Lorrain, out of amity for the author, even came along one day in his 'pall-mall',[1] on a day when I was decked out—and I mean decked out—like a vulgar Bob Walter. That was the general rehearsal, one Friday evening—the day of Venus!—after midnight.

"Having arrived at the theater at quarter to eleven, I was changing in my dressing-room, as frilly as you've known it, when someone knocked on the door, at the very moment when I found myself

in the simple costume of a young beauty wrenched from sleep . . .

"'Don't come in!' I shouted. And to Augustine, my chambermaid: 'Bolt the door. My God! How stupid you are, my girl!'

"But before Augustine had made the slightest movement, the door was vigorously thrown open, and . . . and Thophile, my Thophile of the waterside, in the costume of an electrician, having replaced his

---

brasseries where writers and artists hung out; the Impressionist painter Jean-Louis Forain started out as an illustrator and caricaturist, and was a friend of Joris-Karl Huysmans, Paul Verlaine and Arthur Rimbaud as well as Édouard Manet and Edgar Degas; Henri de Toulouse-Lautrec (1864-1901) alienated from respectable society by virtue of his dwarfism, developed a particular affinity for prostitutes and cabaret dancers, which enabled him to become a unique chronicler of that sector of the Parisian underclass.

1 The reference is slightly enigmatic, but "Pall-Mall" was familiar in Paris at the time as the name of a brand of cigarettes as well as in the title of the Pall Mall Gazette, from which Lorrain probably appropriated it for use in his "Raitif de la Bretonne" diary column.

dunce's cap with a jockey's cap, irrupted into my room clamoring: 'Oh, the slut! Ah, I've found you again! Not without difficulty!'

"Stupefied, alarmed by that invasion, I couldn't think. My head vacillated. Buzzing filled my ears. And Thophile threw himself at my knees, telling me the most implausible of stories, his searches for me all over Paris, and finally, his subterfuge in order to reach me. It was quite simple; he had been put on the track by a poster and had entered the Olympe-Plastique in the capacity of an electrician. Oh, now he would always be here, beside me; nothing could separate us any longer. We would always belong to one another!

"And as, at a sign from me, that imbecile Augustine, misunderstanding, ran to find the stage manager in search of help, my Thophile threw himself on my person and . . ."

"Don't go on; I've understood."

"Yes, but this is the best part. Augustine brought back everyone: the director, the stage managers and artistes, and Jean des Glaïeuls. The Duc d'Arles, my little Duc d'Arles also came in, bringing me a superb opal necklace he had promised me for some time.

"It was then that des Glaïeuls' wicked tongue, understanding at a glance my situation and that of Thophile, murmured in a low voice to Henri Commerce:

"'Nine d'Aubusson is playing the Lady of the Opals externally . . . and internally, ah, Messaline, the Lady of the Opals!'

"And I was thus baptized for three months."

THE MAN FROM BILLANCOURT
(*Le Supplement*, 21 February 1903)

For Marguerite Roesler[1]

"NINE, my dear friend, you keep me in suspense, and exacerbate me even more, with your love story, the display of your joys savored in the company this Thophile of the waterside, who, out of passion for your genteel person, abandoned his mates in Boulogne and became an electrician at the Olympe-Plastique. That knight in a flat cap appears to me to have only existed in your imagination . . . and you're quite imaginative!"

"Not at all," replied Nine d'Aubusson. "I invent nothing. My idyll with Thophile is all that there is of the most veridical. Ah, do you believe that there's only you who could inspire such passions?"

"I don't have that conceit. But you'll have difficulty persuading me that a wolf of the quays might

---

1 "Marguerite Roesler" was a dancer featured regularly in the *Supplement*'s gossip column and lists of performers in 1904-5, sometimes with a *particule* added to her pseudonym.

abandon for amour—simply for amour—his mates on the banks of the Seine. That's because I know that society well. I've frequented it sufficiently. There's only one thing that guides and directs it: *pèze, jonc, blé*—money, that is!"

"But who is telling you otherwise?" said my companion, getting slightly carried away. "Isn't it droll that Fabrice, with his mania for interrupting incessantly . . . ? Let me finish my story; you can argue afterwards."

She formed a significant moue, her moue of a bad-tempered child. I was risking not knowing Nine d'Aubusson's adventure, so I made a decision rapidly not to say another word; and in order to reenter into grace, I leaned over and deposited two kisses on the lady's hand. La Nine smiled. I was forgiven. She continued her story:

"Evidently, there was cause for that infatuation on Thophile's part. During our week of amour in Boulogne, I had not failed to give him a few presents . . . twenty *taches* to pay for his time, all the afternoons he consecrated to excursions on the river. Everyone has to live, and amour doesn't nourish! And on leaving I'd slipped him a banknote to get some smart clothes, as that was his dream. On seeing himself like that from one day to the next, in possession of fifty louis, my Thophile had become intoxicated. Finished, the hard work, only good for dopes! When one is a handsome fellow, like him, one doesn't remain a mariner. The pullets were there to hand, no so?

"And when he ran out of money, he immediately thought of me, whose engagement at the Olympe-Plastique he had learned from the newspapers. To have himself hired as an electrician was child's play for him. And that is how and why Thophile had rushed into my dressing-room and had played me the grand air of passion.

"I understood that the day after that resurrection, merely by the fashion in which the fellow 'borrowed' money from me. And there was no way of avoiding that 'loan'; the little Duc d'Arles would have been alerted to my amours in Boulogne, and he was not a man to forgive. He would have dropped me the day after; and then, you can see my situation from here. Reduced to the two thousand francs a month that Henri Commerce, my hardly-lavish director, was paying me—me, who had a five louis bill every day for flowers from Chez Lion . . .

"Thophile knew all that, and the wretch abused the situation. There were new tappings every day, for eight or ten bullets to bet on the horses or drink with the mates. The entire theater knew the story, except for my lover; the thing was classic. I was no longer living, I dreaded a catastrophe at any minute; it was as if I were suspended over an abyss. And around me, there was no one to advise me, to guide me. Not one friend—and anyway, one knows what female friends are worth!

"Jean des Glaïeuls, the sole being in whom I could have confided, and who would certainly have attempted the impossible to save me, had departed for Bretagne two days after the premiere of *Messaline s'ennuie*, to run around the sailors' dives of Nantes and Saint-Nazaire, from which he sent me, at weekly intervals, letters monstrous in their cynicism.

"I was quite alone, and no one could do anything against my blackmailer. There was the police, but you know that women don't much like going to make their confidences to the Tour Pointue or the station.

"And that infernal life lasted for two months—two months during which I didn't sleep tranquilly for a single hour. *Messaline s'ennuie* obtained a great success, brought Paris flocking, and because of my engagement I was riveted to the Olympe-Plastique, the theater in which my spider came to my dressing-room every evening to suck my blood.

"Oh, the filthy creature, the abominable creature! Twenty times, I offered him a large sum to get rid of him, above all to get back all the little love letters, requests for rendezvous, and others that I'd had the imprudence to write during our week of amour. He accepted the money, returned one of the pieces of paper and kept the rest.

"In the end, madly exasperated, I was perhaps about to play dirty—yes, truly, to kill him—when an adventure brought the situation to an abrupt conclusion.

"That day, Monday 14 January—oh, I shall always remember that date—I had gone to embrace my mother, my poor mother who, in consequence of the bad memories that Boulogne evoked, I had neglected to wish a happy new year. I spent two hours with the worthy old woman and, the weather being splendid and the sky nacreous, the whim took me to return to Paris by boat. I sent my carriage away and embarked bravely on a *bateau-mouche*.

"In addition, I needed distraction, and in spite of the painful, dolorous romance of the previous November, my love of the water hadn't diminished. The water! As transparent as moonstone that day, in the distance it took on precious tints of molten emerald. After the Pont de Billancourt I was so enthused that I got down at the station, planning to go as far as the Auteuil viaduct on foot, very gently, following the river bank.

It was a Monday, as I've told you, and you know what an aspect the Parisian suburb presents on a Monday: all the pipe-smoking boatmen, all the three-card tricksters, everything that lives on vice and sausages, and drinks liters in the wine-merchants in the company of unspeakable whores, the streetwalkers who prowl all the exterior boulevards.

"Amused by the torsos of unemployed butcher-boys who were performing gymnastics in a waste-ground, I stopped on the edge of a fence, and a man's voice murmured against my neck, near the nape:

"'Ah, a lovely kid! I'd rather have that in my bed than a gendarme!'

"I turned round and found myself face to face with a kind of blond Hercules clad in a blouse, with a carter's horsewhip around his neck. Two blue eyes, of the blue loved by Jean des Glaïeuls, illuminated that face. In brief, the ideal conductor of beasts.

"Before I had made the slightest movement, he passed an arm around my waist and said: 'Come and have a glass with me.' And he immediately added: 'One could get oneself killed for such a gonzesse.'

"A mad, absurd idea crossed my mind . . . and without saying a word, I went with the man, who dragged me into a low tavern, made me sit down under an arbor in front of a dusty table with kegs fixed in the ground. A simple hedge separated us from the black causeway that went down to the river.

"The man ordered two kirsch grenadines, then, with his elbows on the table continued to pay me compliments in the language of a tripe-dresser, not without flavor, which were sometimes mingled— alas!—with insipid expressions of romance.

"I told you that a mad, absurd idea had just crossed my mind. 'So,' I said, abruptly, 'you find me lovely— is that true?'

"'Too right!' he replied, with a coarse laugh.

"'And if I asked you to do something—to abolish a man I hate, for example—you wouldn't hesitate?'

"'Surely not . . . especially if there were a recompense.' And he laughed again.

"'Agreed!' I said 'Put it there!'

"I held out my hand, and, looking him in the eyes, I lit the man up entirely."

A WOMAN'S VENGEANCE
(*Le Supplement*, 28 February 1903)

For Sarah Duhamel[1]

"MY plan was formulated, and you've understood immediately, haven't you, my dear?" Nine d'Aubusson explained, lighting her eternal cigarette. "It was necessary for me to avenge myself, and cruelly, on that ignoble ponce . . . and the opportunity was too tempting to foul up."

It's true; she said "foul up." Nine thus brought me out of her story—fundamentally rather banal—of a pretty girl seduced by a fop and falling prey to a ponce, in vaguely literary parlance. Oh, one could well say of my friend that reading had been deadly.

"The handsome lad of the waterside that I had before me, the handsome lad with the blue eyes, was going to rid me of Thophile. I told you: a plan had just been improvised in my head.

---

1 Sarah Duhamel (1873-1926) was a comedienne who appeared in revues in Paris around the turn of the century before going on to appear in numerous short comedy films

66

"I knew that Thophile was spending that day with his mates in Boulogne. Nothing was therefore easier for me than to take my new conquest into the corners where I was sure to find my parasite.

"And that's what I did. I caught the boat again at the Billancourt station, accompanied by my new conquest, eager, tender and attentive. We disembarked at Boulogne and started running around the quayside taverns.

"Oh, I swear to you that our couple did not lack a touch of the picturesque. No, but you can see me from here, hanging on the arm of that big fellow, murmuring stimulating words in his ear, intoxicating him with promises and telling him his role—to wit, falling on Thophile with arms bent, raining blows upon him, and taking by force the little wallet that never quit him, the little wallet that contained my imprudent love letters.

"The fellow swore to me anything I wished. He looked good like that, clenching his fists, his blue eyes lighting up with a joy of carnage and lust!

"Night fell, and we were still roaming the guinguettes. I saluted dubious acquaintances, I asked after Thophile. No one had seen him—no one at all! It was despairing, and I despaired completely. It would be necessary for me to return to Paris. I was furious.

"We went into the last tavern, and finally, I learned there from the very mouth of one of his mates, that Thophile had just left, in order to go along the bank toward Billancourt.

"I gave the man a hundred sous and went out precipitately, followed by my lover, who was brandishing his whip in a threatening manner.

"Outside, it was pitch dark, a black night hardly pricked, in a few places, by meager lights, a true January night of melodrama, a night for a fifth act at the Ambigu . . .

"A form was zigzagging before me on the bank. That was Thophile, a little drunk, singing a ditty. I approached him, making a sign to my companion to follow me at a stealthy pace, and only to intervene on my signal.

"I arrived at Thophile. 'Well, well, what are you doing here?' I asked him, in an almost amicable tone.

"'And you?' replied the barbet.

"'Me? I've just been to see Maman, and by the way, she's advised me strongly not to see you any more . . . My lover will end up discovering the pot of roses one day, and I'll be fresh . . . That's why, Thophile, it's better for my tranquility that no one sees me dragging you in my entourage any longer, especially around my dressing-room at the Olympe-Plastique.'

"'There was a time,' Thophile mocked, "when you had regard for me. It would be necessary to be rudely stupid to let go of such a pretty kid like that, and from such a height. You wouldn't want that, my *bibiche*. I'm not yet done!"

"'However, it's necessary that we separate; this adventure has lasted too long. Return the letters to me, and go away.'

"'No, but you see, I'm not yet drunk enough. Then again, all that is rubbish. Come here so I can kiss you, and take my arm!'

"At the same time, Thophile tried to put his arms around me.

"That was too much for my lover; he couldn't contain himself any longer. With one bound he was beside Thophile, and with his powerful hand, open like a claw, he gripped the throat of my blackmailer. He squeezed, squeezed hard enough to choke him. The other weakened. Inarticulate sounds emerged from his throat, the grunts of a beast having its throat cut. And Thophile fell. I precipitated myself upon him, snapped the buttons of his overcoat and took possession of the wallet. Then, leaping to my feet, I ran straight ahead, at hazard, leaving the two men to continue their fight.

"I had recovered my tranquility."

La Nine interrupted herself.

"And the consequence of your adventure?" I asked her.

"There was no consequence," Nine replied. "I was never to see Thophile again."

"Good! And your savior? You didn't worry about him? That isn't good. You'd contracted a debt to that man. Nine, my dear Nine, you ought to have acquitted yourself."

"Bah!" said the pretty girl, shrugging her shoulders lightly. "If we had to acquit all the debts that we contract, where would we be?"

69

"Perhaps you're right. But you say that Thophile never gave you his news again?"

"Never."

"He didn't write to you, didn't threaten you, didn't try to trouble your life?"

"Not in any fashion."

"That's very strange, and not in the habits of those messieurs. I don't understand . . ."

"You will."

"I'd like nothing better."

"A week later, while scanning the newspapers, I read that the cadavers of two individuals, tightly enlaced, had just been fished out of the river at Boulogne. You can guess who those two individuals were."

"Damn! Thophile and your lover from Billancourt."

"Yes, them. In their bloody struggle they had fallen from the height of the bank into the river, and into death.

"That ought to explain to you, my dear Fabrice, why the name of Billancourt, dropped by you a little while ago into the conversation in the Café de Paris, gave me something of a chill."

AT THE PONT D'IÉNA
(*Le Supplement*, 7 March 1903)

For Derminy[1]

"LOVE and death—but it's very Ambigu-Comique, your adventure, even too Ambigu. I don't like your ending: two men who die for a woman, that's in the worst bad taste nowadays. Then too, you nurse your effects too much."

And, satisfied by having rebuked Nine d'Aubusson in my turn, I smiled. She was doubtless about to respond to me with some amenity when the carriage stopped dead at the entrance to the Pont d'Iéna, so suddenly and so sharply that I leapt out of the fiacre and joined the coachman, who had also leapt down from his seat.

"Well, coachman, what's the matter."

"My horse has gone lame, Monsieur."

"Bah!"

---

1 Marthe Derminy was another actress who eventually made a name for herself in movies (long after the present story was published), and was also featured on numerous picture postcards.

"See for yourself." And the man went on, grumbling: "Well, after three trots like that, it's not surprising. Traveling since six o'clock in the evening from Madame's house in the Rue Franklin, at the top of a slope as stiff as any, until such an hour, five o'clock in the morning . . . a horse needs constancy, you know!"

"You're saying things, my friend . . ."

"I'm saying true things. What kind of life is it, dragging poor coachmen around all night, into dirty corners of Paris like Grenelle! Not to mention that Madame and you have such fine acquaintances!"

"Shut it!" howled La Nine, dear Nine d'Aubusson, emerging from the fiacre, forgetting all literature and resuming momentarily her voice of childhood and the river bank. Then she went on: "Give him some money and tell the animal to get lost!"

"As you wish, dear friend—only, let me remind you that the water's edge, at this hour of the night, isn't very safe . . ."

The coachman interrupted me. "Since I've told you that my horse has just gone lame . . ."

"Yes," Nine cut him off, "since he's told you that his horse has just gone lame! Pay the coachman off. The fellow makes me sick."

There was no doubt about it; the waterside had changed my Nine!

I therefore paid the coachman, and the latter no sooner had his money than he climbed back on his seat, lifted up his horse with a whiplash, and the beast, evidently no more lame than me, set off flat out, if I dare risk that figure of speech.

I could not get over it. Nor did Nine. It was only five minutes later that, amused at having fallen into the trap, we burst out laughing.

Then I said: "My dear Nine, that's not all. What are we going to do?"

"Whatever you like."

"That's not an answer. I proposed to you to go and see the sunrise in the heart of the Parisian suburbs, but I believe that we'll have to renounce that project. I can't see you walking all night along the river bank. Encounters here, for sometimes being amorous, aren't always deprived of a dangerous character."

"You're giving up, then?"

"I'm not giving up, but . . ."

"But what? What are you saying? It's evident that you're weakening. Do you call yourself a man?"

"At times, yes, my dear."

With that, we started laughing again. And I swear to you that we must have had a rather bizarre aspect, Nine and I, for any passer-by who might have perceived us there, laughing in bursts, like kids, at five o'clock in the morning next to the Pont d'Iéna.

But all things, and all actions, have their time; and when our fit of laughter had passed, the question of how we were going to employ the end of our night presented itself again in all its beauty.

"In truth," declared Nine, "since Hazard, the god of ladies of amour and artistes, doesn't want us to go and drink milk at Meudon, I'm going home . . ."

"It's the voice of reason that is speaking through your mouth, Nine."

"Let me finish. I'm going home and you're going to accompany me."

"To your house?"

"To my house."

"You can't think so! What about your lover . . . what will he say when he hears that you've offered me hospitality at five o'clock in the morning?"

"My lover? I don't give a **** about him."

She uttered the word flatly. Then she continued: "What do you expect him to say? He knows you, and your reputation . . . and he knows very well, like everyone else, that I'm only your type for conversation. Outside of conversation, nothing exists between us. We've abandoned the metaphorical bagatelle."

"Allow me to deplore it."

"Get away, joker! You're not saying what you're thinking. Anyway, let's go. Are you coming?"

"Since you demand it."

"I command it!"

"How you employ the big words!"

The fact is that she had taken my arm and she abducted me, in a cavalier fashion. The gates of the Trocadéro being closed, we resigned ourselves to going around the heavy edifice, which, in the clear night, extended its two arms desperately toward the clouds.

Madame d'Aubusson lived in a delightful ground-floor apartment in the Rue Franklin, near the corner of the Place du Trocadéro, and less than ten minutes after making our decision, we penetrated into the actress' home—and that without waking the concierge; we simply climbed in through a window!

It was charming, in the latest Grand-Guignol style. One might have thought that we were in a play by Mirbeau.

The scratch of a match on the box, a lamp lit, the window reclosed, and Nine and I found ourselves in a tête-à-tête in the lady's very bedroom, a bedroom in the latest modern style, a modern style organized by Georges de Feure,[1] with supple and graceful furniture, especially a bed, a low bed inviting slumber and amour, a bed like an altar of sensuality.

Nine unhooked herself, glad after all to find herself at home, and while I pretended discreetly to be interested in a thousand-and-one trinkets that trailed over the sideboards, tables and the mantelpiece, and peered at the portraits of cavaliers, not all of whom had a grand allure, but all of whose silhouettes I had seen in Sem's album, the dear child, rid of her dress and underskirt, put on the most improbable of peignoirs, pale green and decorated with arachnean lace.

That done, turning back to me, she released yet another burst of crazy laughter, threw herself on her bed, lit another inevitable cigarette, and her musical voice launched at me: "My dear Fabrice, I'm all stories tonight. That doesn't bore you?"

"You're joking."

"Really?"

"I assure you."

---

1 The art nouveau pioneer "Georges de Feure" (George van Sluijters, 1868-1943) designed furniture as well as theatrical sets and a famous poster for the Folies Bergère depicting the dancer Jane Derval.

"Well, in that case, I'll continue. I'll tell you something astonishing, miraculous, an incredible adventure . . . and if you refuse to believe it, I'll furnish you with proofs."

"It's as extraordinary as that?"

"Even more than that."

"You're scaring me. Speak, quickly . . ."

"I'm going to tell you a love story that happened to Jean des Glaïeuls."

"Eh?"

"Precisely. A story of amour, and normal amour, that happened to Jean des Glaïeuls—Jean de Glaïeuls the invert, the invert *par excellence*, the amoral individual about which we've talked so much this evening."

"You interest me to the highest degree, of course. Jean des Glaïeuls in love with a woman . . . I'm listening."

THE BIZARRE ADVENTURE
(*Le Supplement*, 14 March 1903)

"A veritable story of normal amour that happened to Jean des Glaïeuls! Truly, my dear, it's necessary that it be you in order for me to burst out laughing. Jean des Glaïeuls in love, him, the invert *par excellence*, as I said to you two minutes ago, the strange young man about whom nothing is known except for his passion for spiders, flowers, jewels and lace, the monsieur who always wears too many pearl and ruby rings, and whose equivocal adventures along the river bank, in Billancourt and Grenelle, and also in the vicinity of the Gobelins, have fed the gossip columns for so many years . . . Jean des Glaïeuls, smitten with rubustnesses—and what robustnesses—throwing himself into a romance *à deux* like anyone else . . . that beats me . . . oh, yes!"

"And you're right, for our friend has never been reputed to ruin himself with women.

"You know that it's been claimed for a long time that he pays butcher-boys double—the word is Scholl's."[1]

---

1 The reference is to the recently-deceased journalist Aurélian

"It's not new, then, it's second hand. And more-over, I believe it applies poorly to our friend. Let's say that he simply pays them and leave it at that; for I dare to affirm to you that Jean des Glaïeuls is worth more than his singular reputation."

"What do you mean by that?"

"I mean that his bizarre amours are much exagger-ated. Evidently, des Glaïeuls isn't a normal monsieur, but from that to making him the monster that people want to impose on our minds is a long step. His bad reputation is merited, but it seems to me to be a little magnified . . .

"And so jealously maintained by his entourage, vague friends of the boulevard, editorial offices and the theater . . . and also by himself. It doesn't displease him to cultivate his legend himself. I've sensed that for a long time."

"And you're right. My story, or rather history, will demonstrate it to you."

Nine d'Aubusson shook her cigarette; then, doubt-less feeling ill at ease in her horizontal position on her bed, she got up, leapt to the floor and threw herself, legs crossed, into an armchair. Having done that, she began her story.

"It was last year, in spring—a painful and muddy spring, during which I had to keep to my room. Jean des Glaïeuls was then having a little piece rehearsed, *Fleurs de trimard*, due to his collaboration with Adhémar Le Menestrier, the well-known dramatic author to whom we owe such admirable adaptations.

Scholl (1833-1902), renowned for his satirical chronicles of Parisian life.

"Not a week went by when des Glaïeuls didn't come to see me, to obtain my news and to chat. He always arrived in the morning, at about eleven o'clock, and surprised me in bed. And we then had delightful conversations until lunch time, about clothes, gems and gossip—especially gossip, for he adores that sort of exercise, and isn't at all reluctant to create it. Personally, I love that young man in the morning. He has just read the newspapers; his head is stuffed with all the interesting news items, and he lists them with apt comments. In brief, he's my living gazette and, I admit it, how substantial!

"So, one morning in March, a morning even muddier than all the rest, true Baudelairean weather

In which everything is misty
In which the memory
Wanders under a sky of soot,

to serve you up three decadent lines—a morning in March, then, when des Glaïeuls, whom I hadn't seen for a week, arrived, and Augustine, my chambermaid, who had orders, introduced him into my room.

"He let himself fall rather than sitting down into the armchair where you are sitting at this moment, and in a conceited voice, a slightly veiled voice, with his eyes extinct, he declared to me: 'Oh, my dear friend, what a delightful night.'

"'Go on, then, tell me about it,' I said, amused. 'I assume that you've had an adventure.'

"'And what an adventure,' he went on. 'But permit me to repair the disorder of my costume somewhat.

And excuse my nocturnal—more than nocturnal—linen. First, have you a button-hook? My boots are unbuttoned and I dare not, decently, remain before you a moment longer in this state of disarray . . .'

"I directed him to the dressing-cabinet. He precipitated himself into it, buttoned himself up, even took the care of his person as far as having a wash and powdering himself with my own powder—I forgive him everything; he knows that, and abuses it—and returned to collapse in the armchair."

"'Well, what about the adventure?'

"'Here it is, and here's the object of it.'

"With that, my des Glaïeuls takes out of his wallet a wretched fairground photograph and holds it out to me. The portrait was that of a young mariner, twenty years old at the most, of Herculean stature, with a child-like face. Two guttersnipe eyes were laughing in that innocent head, as if aureoled by a beret tilted like an acrobat's.

"'How do you like him?' said des Glaüieuls, smiling with an ever more conceited expression.

"'Not bad.'

"'Isn't he? He doesn't say anything to you?'

"'In truth, no.'

"'Well, my dear, you're wrong. You don't understand much about masculine beauty. Let me tell you that in passing.'

"I was about to respond hotly when des Glaïeuls, taking back the photograph, declaimed: 'But look at those eyes and that benevolent face. Come on, Nine, you haven't looked properly.'

"Then he put the photograph back in his wallet. 'And what an amiable companion,' he continued. Can you imagine that I made his acquaintance yesterday, at the exit from my rehearsal of *Fleurs de trimard*. He'd come to wait for one of my interpreters, Gabrielle Mina, a funny girl with the air of a Jeanne d'Arc of the fortifs. And as that rascally and cynical gamine pleases me infinitely, and as the mariner pleased me more with her, I found nothing better to do than take them to dinner in a restaurant in the Rue Saint-Lazare, where I'm sufficiently well known to permit myself a few eccentricities.

"'In fact, I sat down there sandwiched between those two fresh complexions and I had the couple tell me rather lewd stories. They were a chance couple, and I quickly had the explanation of it: one of those unions that stick and come apart that are sketched every day, for forty-eight hours, in Paris.

"'After dinner, Gabrielle Mina having to rejoin a meager and aged maintainer, left us and I found myself alone, tête-à-tête with Jean-Marie—that was his name. My evening being free, I decided immediately to show that Breton Paris by night—for he's a Breton from Lorient. I dragged him from the Folies Bergère to Olympia, and at the Casino, at midnight, I exhibited him triumphantly in a bar near the Opéra; and at two o'clock in the morning, the mariner was drunk on light, music and alcohol. I took him to a furnished hotel I know, and I . . .'

"'Don't go on!'

"I interrupted Jean des Glaïeuls at the moment when, carried away, he was about to say something stupid. He undermined it anyway with a fatigued and satisfied smile, if I might express myself thus. Then, dabbing his forehead with a handkerchief over-furnished with lace, he repeated, in exclamation, and twice: 'What a night, my dear! What a night!'

"But there was too much affectation in his words. It wasn't the first time that Jean des Glaïeuls had made me such bizarre confidences. I'd heard many others. But this time, I don't know why, a doubt rose up within me. That excessively theatrical arrival, the coup of the unbuttoned boots and the unarranged costume, and my friend's 'more fatigued than natural' air all seemed to me to be devoid of sincerity. I sniffed deception. Was Jean des Glaïeuls trying to put one over on me?

"'And Jean-Marie is downstairs, in a carriage,' Jean des Glaïeuls finished. 'Would you like to see him before I take him back to his legitimate owner?'

"That was the bouquet. I leapt to the bottom of the bed, asked our friend to spend a minute in the adjoining dining room, under a futile pretext, went to the window, lifted a corner of the curtain, and did indeed observe the presence of a fiacre . . . but a pale ringed hand emerged from the portière, a woman's hand . . .

"Jean des Glaïeuls was bragging; his pseudo-matelot was a woman. But why that deception? With what goal?

"I was to learn that a few days later."

HIS MISTRESS
(*Le Supplement*, 21 March 1903)

"WELL, yes," Nine d'Aubusson continued, "the explanation of Jean des Glaïeuls' boasting was given to me a few days later. I perceived the mystery so jealously guarded and so awkwardly announced by Jean des Glaïeuls—Jean des Glaïeuls, who would have done better to keep quiet, since he wanted to conserve in my eyes his dubious aureole of a bardash."

La Nine said *bardash*; she was resuming her literary tint.

"But as I told you, this time, it didn't work; and I had reason for doubt!

"A fortnight after des Glaïeuls' little performance, the excessively pretty young man dined at my house: a very simple and very intimate dinner; just my lover, the Duc d'Arles, and Jane de Nancy, a Jane de Nancy that would have been a joy for you to contemplate, as a lover of gems; a Jane de Nancy whose fingers were studded with emeralds of a mysterious water, as if shaded by fresh verdure.

"Our friend seemed exhausted, worn out, that evening, but with an exhaustion that I was not accustomed to seeing. It was not the blissful and valiant lassitude that he loved to display at my *petit levers*, the fatigue of the Monsieur who has vices and is pleased that people talk about them. No, he offered me instead the aspect of a Monsieur who has gone astray in a very bourgeois manner for a few hours in the arms of a lady.

"I knew that exhaustion from having observed it so much. A woman's kisses do not fatigue in the same way as a man's, the latter slake a thirst but still leave one full of ardor and the desire for *something else* . . . the former leave one broken, dead of fatigue, devoid of desire and joy, for woman is bitter and her arms are chains, whereas man . . . but you're not smoking?"

Nine interrupted herself, got up, fetched blond cigarettes from a side-table and passed them to me.

"No thank you, not for me. I have a slight sore throat."

"A little—very little—pipe of Indian hemp, then? I have a whole packet, which Gustave de Lautrémont—you know, my delightfully ironic poet—brought me a few days ago."[1]

"Thanks again, my dear friend, but I've promised the Faculty to abandon all narcotics, and I like to keep all my promises . . . especially those."

---

1 Jean Lorrain's friend Gabriel de Lautrec (1867-1938) boasted of having composed most of his *Poems en prose* (1898) under the influence of hashish.

"No more ether, then, and no more morphine? But that's a conversion!"

"As you say, it's a conversion. And then, I don't want to have my belly opened again on the pretext of peritonitis. I suffered too much last year, on my back in my bed with my pregnant woman's belly imprisoned in ice! But go on with your story . . . and smoke for two!"

She lit her fifth cigarette of the evening—at least—crossed her legs again and then continued her story.

"In truth, yes, Jean des Glaïeuls was exhausted and morose; and after dinner, when we went into the drawing room, Jane sat down at the piano and launched her street-urchin voice into the refrain of your song *Le Dompteur*:

> *He's so chic in his cream costume*
> *That I've sworn to myself*
> *That he'll be my adored little man*
> *For as long as he wants, even always;*
> *I have him in my blood, the tamer I love!*

"He got up abruptly, as if that song had reminded him of his misadventure with the handsome Drack, and, coming to me, he declared:

"'I'm going; will you excuse me?'

"'What, already?'

"'It's necessary.'

"'But it's only half past ten. Come on, stay with us, dear friend.'

"'Half past ten? Damn! I only just have time to get there . . .'

"'Where?'

"'You're very curious.'

"'I'm a woman. Where are you going?"

"'To a rendezvous.'

"'Amorous?'

"'Perhaps.'

"'That's not a response: *Perhaps*. Is it an amorous rendezvous, yes or no?'

"'In which sex?' interrogated Jane de Nancy, coming closer. And as Jean des Glaïeuls didn't respond, she went on: 'Oh, you can tell us. We have no desire to throw you on the griddle, you know.'

"Then he had an adorably conceited smile, and he launched at me, only me, while looking at me: 'I'm continuing my story of the mariner.'

"Then, a salute, and he left.

"I followed him as far as the entrance door, where Augustine helped him to put on his pelisse. And, determined to have an explanation on the subject of that immense lie, I was about to tell him that I was not his dupe, that I knew perfectly well that the pseudo-matelot was quite simply and honestly a person of the opposite sex to his own when . . . when I suddenly read in des Glaïeuls' face a great, immense sadness. It was like a veil of crepe fallen over a sunlit landscape.

"Jean des Glaïeuls took my hand, deposited thereon a kiss of homage and farewell, and, turning on his heels, quit my abode before, mute with surprise, I had time to address the slightest question to him.

"I stood there as if petrified. Jean des Glaïeuls sad! Him, the ironist, the man of ferocious words! Positively, I couldn't get over it.

"Augustine tugged the sleeve of my peignoir, with the fine familiarity that you know and of which I've never been able to cure her during the six years she's been in my service.

"'Madame!'

"'What?'

"'It's this letter and this piece of paper that have just fallen from Monsieur des Glaïeuls' pocket.'

"At the same time, she handed me a letter, on stiff paper the color of *cuisse de nymph émue*[1] and a fragment of a leaf of foolscap. I deciphered the fragment covered in Jean des Glaïeuls' handwriting. They were lines of poetry, scratched out, having been bungled. Here they are; I've conserved them."

Nine d'Aubussion rummaged in a little box among an accumulation of dried flowers, portraits, yellow pieces of paper and locks of hair, all shades from black to blond. From that reliquary of amour, in which my indiscreet eyes glimpsed even more bizarre things—a cigarette-roller; a domino (double six) and a cross of the Légion d'honneur—she brought out a piece of paper, which she handed to me.

In the midst of erasures, I read these lines:

---

1 *Cuisse de nymphe émue* [thigh of an emotional nymph] was the trade name of a popular variety of pink paint, adapted from that of a variety of rose.

. . . But my life is dishonored;
Why did I not encounter you
In the tender May of my spring?
We would have lived good times,
And my soul, forever wounded
Would have put you in my thoughts!

And there was also, further down the page, after other erasures:

. . . O perfumed flower
Forgotten by the road,
Mina, beloved mistress,
I still desire your hand.
O Lord, let live again
For a day, the good times;
Sing again, O my youth,
The verses of your twenty years!

"As for the letter, which I have mislaid," Nine d'Aubussion continued, "it only contained these simple words: *I want you to come to the theater this evening at eleven o'clock.* It was signed *Gabrielle Mina.*

"Suddenly, I understood everything. That Gabrielle Mina was des Glaïeuls' passion, his pseudo-matelot. And it was out of shame, an imbecile shame, that our friend did not want anyone to suspect his normal amour, it was out of shame that he had recounted an absurd adventure to me.

"That was really it. I had discovered everything. But it would not be said that des Glaïeuls put one over on me. No, never in this life. The others, yes, he could tell them all the stories that it pleased him to invent . . .

"My resolution was made. I swore not to be a dupe in his eyes.

"I went back to the drawing room and pretexted a sudden illness to the Duc d'Arles. Being assured in that regard of the complicity of Jane de Nancy, in whom I have every confidence, I persuaded my lover to take my friend home. He accepted eagerly, glad—I have since discovered—to find therein an opportunity to go and play cards at the club. The folly of gambling, which led him you-know-where, was beginning to take hold of him at that time. And Jane de Nancy, mistaking my purpose, murmured in my ear: 'Enjoy yourself!'

"Left alone, I dressed in haste, to the great alarm of Augustine, who had rarely seen me as prompt. Judge for yourself, in fact: a quarter of an hour later, I threw myself into a fiacre on the Place du Trocadéro, and the coachman, stimulated by the promise of a big tip, whipped his horse with a mighty arm, to employ a popular expression. Eleven o'clock had only just chimed when I presented myself at the office of the little theater where *Fleurs de trimard*, Jean des Glaïeuls' play, was being performed.

"In the office, recognized by an amiable young man, a journalist and the secretary of the theater, I was welcomed as a veritable queen of the boards. The director offered me a box, one of three that his hall possessed, and the young secretary offered me his arm. I accepted both, while begging those messieurs to keep my visit secret and not to divulge it to anyone, especially Jean des Glaïeuls. They made me that promise.

"From the box, on the first floor—a box that over-looked the whole of the hall and the stage, in which one could not be seen—I searched the ranks of arm-chairs with my gaze, and ended up discovering Jean des Glaïeuls in the first row.

"The play had scarcely begun. It was a matter of a study of the mores of the society of vagabonds and tramps. There was a camp of bohemians and bandits. It must have been piquant, because the audience seemed to be keenly interested.

"Abruptly, a young woman, very 'Jeanne'Arc of the fortifs,' as my friend had depicted her, Gabrielle Mina, came on stage. Coiffed à la Cléo, her head high and her body slim, devoid of hips, almost the body of a little boy, that Gabrielle Mina, with her hoarse voice of a vicious schoolboy, was a type, and what a type!—a true flower of vice doubtless grown in some corner of Montmartre, or even Saint-Ouen.

"'That's our star,' the young secretary assured me.

"'Ah! Well, you know, for a star she isn't very shiny—or, rather, her glare is distinctly fake. Can one sport such tinsel and such garish pieces of glass!'

"The fact is that Gabrielle Mina, in her desire to play the star completely, was quite ridiculous with her exhibition of bazaar jewelry. Blue, white, red and green glassware covered her hands, her arms and her breast; it was touching by virtue of being grotesque, for the young person was incarnating a gypsy girl.

"However, I had to recognize that she was playing her role adroitly. For me, who has worked with Jean des Glaïeuls, I sensed very clearly that he had 'passed that way.' I recognized his method, his fashion of comprehending roles, his stage-setting, all of his 'stagecraft'—thanks to which he had arrived at giving a semblance of talent to so many demoiselles of the Palais de Glace and elsewhere who become actresses because they imagine that the stage is a prolongation of the sidewalk."

Nine d'Aubusson paused, and I smiled faintly—unknown to her.

Seriously, by the fashion in which La Nine judged her contemporaries, one sensed that the lady of amour believed that she was an artiste, and what an artiste—without any doubt the equal of Sarah Bernhardt, Gabrielle Réjane and Jeanne Granier.

She continued: "When the act concluded, resolved to catch the amorous couple at their exit from the theater in order for me to pay des Glaïeuls back, I was getting ready to leave, when the young secretary proposed to let me visit the wings. I accept, counting on hazard to bring about a denouement—I did not know what, or of what genre . . .

"And we penetrated the wings, going up on to the 'plateau,' which was rather nicely fitted out, in truth, and descending into the corridor of the dressing-rooms.

"And it was then that I heard this brief dialogue of two voices, that of des Glaïeuls and that of Gabrielle Mina:

"'Why did you arrive five minutes late?'

"'I was dining with my mother.'

"'That's not a reason.'

"'I promise you, my dear, not to do it again. Are you going to kiss me? Don't scold me—I love you so much.'

"I took a couple of steps forward, and through the door of the dressing-room, which stood ajar, I discovered des Glaïeuls in the classic pose of the petrified lover, on his knees, at the feet of the Jeanne d'Arc of the fortifs.

"He turned round, perceived me, and a blush rose to his face; he stood up and, abruptly making a decision, superbly casual, he launched at me:

"'You, here, my dear Nine d'Aubusson? By what chance? Permit me to introduce to you Mademoiselle Gabrielle Mina, my mistress!'

"And that while two large tears—of shame and vanquished pride—descended slowly over the cheeks of the man of joy reverted in spite of everything, and in spite of himself, to normal amour."

AMOROUS TRINITY
(*Le Supplement*, 28 March 1903)

"'IF I dance for you, you'll come?'

"'How much will you give me?'

"'A hundred sous.'

"'Get away, humbug!'

"'A petit louis?'

"'Come on, love!'

"And it's that Marseillais dialogue—of the warm streets of Old Marseille—that Gabrielle Mina served us, at my house, until the day after the famous evening of *Fleurs de trimard*. Yes, exactly, at my house! I had invited the couple, Jean des Glaïeuls and his mistress, to come and share my dinner, informally, as comrades. A breakfast-dinner, as the populace say, at five o'clock in the evening, for Mina was due on stage at nine; the child needed time to dress.

"The little actress and I had immediately become friends the previous evening, while taking a snack: friends as much as we could be to one another. Certainly, at first, she had appeared ridiculous to me in her harness of fake gemstones, but she gained singularly in becoming known. And then, it amused me to play amity a little with that girl who, having eaten the heart of Jean des Glaïeuls, was avenging us all by finally making known to that monster the power of Woman!

"Des Glaïeuls! He put on quite a face at that dinner! No, but it was pitiful! He had tried hard to chat with me, to explain his soul by attributing that amour to literature; he had been, he said, caught by his passion for the esthetic, Beauty with a capital B, etc., etc. . . . a load of nonsense that he had come to serve me that morning when I got up, and to which I had only responded with a: 'Charming, your sailor! So I'll catch you again in a few hours!'

"He smiled, heartbroken by my small vengeance, left, and came to dinner. And it was at the end of dinner that Gabrielle Mina, somewhat lit up by a few glasses of wine, brought out her dialogue for me:

"'If I dance for you, you'll come?' etc.

"She told me about her existence of adventures—rather meager adventures, in fact—an entire life of a little girl whose Maman knew houses where they like green fruit . . . That Mina had been, from twelve to fifteen, in Paris and on the Côte, a gamine playing vicious gamines, with a virginal air and a pigtail, under the guidance of Madame Mère. Then, on leaving that inferno, she had fallen into the arms of Brestois, the wrestler, so well known on the racecourses and to young women in need of biceps to defend them, Brestois, who had been her first true lover, in all the beauty of the magical word *lover*.

"That Brestois, had she worked hard enough for him, trailing around the music halls of Paris from the end of September to January? Then, beating the Côte until March and coming back to drain Paris until the Grand Prix, to depart again to mint money with her body on the beaches of Normandy! Oh, the hard métier of prostitution, the sickening of those couplings at so much an hour, a day or a month, the ignominy of that insane lust! And at twenty she had known all that, partying at twenty louis a night in Monte Carlo, at times when she exhibited herself in fifty-thousand-franc costumes, and sad encounters in La Villette at forty sous a quarter of an hour.[1] She had known all that, as if in a dream, she had harvested all her youth to make an income for her mother, and then for a ponce!

"Today, released by Brestois, who had found a more advantageous scheme, she had fallen back in Paris, and finally, weary of partying, a partying she had not been able to understand, like so many of her peers—for my dear, knowing how to party, to arrive at figuring in the Feast, is a whole art!—today, that heartless gamine, that soul of mud had improvised herself as an actress, because an adroit 'manager' had been able to indoctrinate her to the point of making her sign a three-year engagement, at a hundred and fifty francs a month and a ten thousand franc indemnity!

---

1 La Villette is nowadays the site of a large park, but when the story was written it was still notorious for its abattoir and meat market.

"And it was in the course of rehearsals that Jean des Glaïeuls had got stuck on her, stuck like a schoolboy, but in that, I could now perceive nothing but the fashions of the ex-man-woman.

"And she, seduced, swollen with pride at the thought of playing a role—and the principal role—in the play by Jean des Glaïeuls and Adhémar Le Menestrier, flattered in seeing de Glaïeuls cajole her, give her lessons and become a little her lover, she treated him like an ordinary lover . . . who did not pay!

"In truth, yes, that was what Jean des Glaïeuls was for Gabrielle Mina of the fake jewels: the little gigolo who doesn't pay, of a poor man's Otero!

"And that was where the excessively pretty fellow had fallen, the abnormal so often cited as the type specimen of inverts, the writer of risqué tales that all the queens of the Fête read!"

Nine d'Aubusson interrupted herself again and relit her extinct cigarette.

I took advantage of that to proclaim: "My dear, in spite of the proofs that you promised me, des Glaïeuls' letters and his verses, which I need to see, in spite of all that, I have difficulty believing all of your story. And 'difficulty' appears to me to be generous; most, not to say all, of our friends would shrug their shoulders!"

Nine immediately became incensed.

"But the proofs, I still have them, and you're going to continue to see them! I'm not improvising at hazard. This story is veridical. There are facts, stories that aren't invented . . . look!"

She rummaged again in the famous casket, brought out letters, photographs and bouquets, all wrapped in pink ribbon, and showed me the package.

"Look, here they are, the proofs! Look at this portrait . . . these portraits!"

I took the photographs. First there was Jean des Glaïeuls, his round face, his blue eyes, in which an eternal spring of sadness seemed to be weeping, his broad and high forehead, straddled by oak-root tresses. Nothing was sadder than that face; there was agony and death in it, and in spite of the sarcasm legible in the mouth, the sharply-designed chin, and even the triumphant flower in the buttonhole, the photograph revealed a despair, a terrifying decline. It was definitely the face of a being whom a life of excess, and excess of all kinds, had fatigued and almost abolished; it was definitely the man whom all Paris has known, seen, and tried to dissect without being able to succeed in doing so, the man who has been found in all alcoves of men and women and who, until now, has given more than the impression of a vicious individual, that of a bad angel of anguish. Truly, I found in confrontation with that photograph the disturbance that seized me every time my eyes beheld certain heads marked by degeneracy.

The other photograph was that of a woman, Gabrielle Mina, and a Gabrielle Mina of theatrical appearance—naturally! She must have been inspired, in striking that pose by that attitude of Christ crowned with thorns that Madame Sarah Bernhardt has rendered familiar to us: the eyes raised to heaven rather than to the true heaven of the bed; her mouth and the hands at prayer, she offered the spectacle of an understudy of Max[1] in a religious drama by Edmond Rostand, a Samaritan for girls' schools. In spite of all that pretence, the demoiselle's face remained rascally. I rediscovered there traces of the vice and poverty of the Parisian faubourgs, the brazen rascality of people who have nothing to lose. La Villette and La Chapelle give us those girls, doubtless in order that Gavarni[2] can form the eternal legend, addressed to the sons of the bourgeois: *Beware of our daughters!*

Another portrait of Gabrielle Mina showed her as Biblical as the previous one, but this time it was a mask of Salome, a bewitching mask, with her eyes bright and wide open, a gaze that seemed to be stealing something of you, so lightly, in passing, as one picks a flower with the fingertips; a Salome with two chrysanthemums in her hair, lying in wait like spiders above the ears: a Salome of the fortifs, of whom Oscar Wilde never dreamed.

I was about to look at the fourth print when Nine d'Aubusson snatched it from my hands with a curt gesture.

"No, not that one!"

"Why not?"

---

1 The celebrated actor Édouard de Max (1869-1924) made his name playing male leads in tragedies; off-stage, he advertised his homosexuality flamboyantly. He appeared on stage in the nude in Beziers in Gabriel Fauré's Wagneresque *Prométhée* (1900), with a libretto by Jean Lorrain and André-Ferdinand Herold, but the censor would not allow it in Paris.
2 The illustrator "Paul Gavarni" (Sulpice Chevalier, 1804-1866), famous as the lead caricaturist for *Le Charivari*.

"Because . . ."

"Because what?"

"Because it isn't to be seen."

"Why give it to me, then?"

"It was a mistake."

"Mistake or not, you've passed me that photograph in order for me to cast an eye over it. I want to see it."

I was still holding on to the cardboard forcefully, one end of which Nine was also holding.

"In fact," she added, "you can look at it. With you, that has no importance. You're discretion itself—at least, you're reputed to be. Look at it at your ease, then; it will advance my story."

She abandoned the card to me.

And the card revealed a group, Jean des Glaïeuls in the middle, his eternal soft hat lowered over his eyes, his hands laden with rings and an expression more flower-girl than ever. By his sides, their heads inclined over his shoulders, were Gabrielle Mina and . . . Nine Aubusson. Yes, Nine Aubusson herself, and her idol's eyes, also departing into Paradise.

"Amorous trinity!" I couldn't help saying. "My dear Nine, now I absolutely must have the end of your story!"

GABRIELLE MINA
(*Le Supplement*, 4 April 1903)

"AMOROUS trinity! Don't believe a word of it!" exclaimed Nine d'Aubusson, into whose hands I abandoned the photograph.

"However, dear friend, your attitude and that of Gabrielle Mina, your nonchalant heads on Jean des Glaïeuls' shoulders, that entire pose of tender and languid sensuality . . ."

"Pure jest!" the actress interrupted. "That photograph was taken on a day of roaming in a fairground in the Boulevard d'Italie, to which the young man of joy had dragged us both one afternoon."

"So you were in his seraglio . . ."

"Not at all! I was continuing my friendship with Jean des Glaïeuls and I was interested in Gabrielle Mina. Then again, to tell you the whole truth, the couple intrigued me singularly, all the more singularly because of the demoiselle's demi-confidences and quarter-confidences. I understood that she had skirted the shores of Lesbos more than once."

"Get away!"

"It's as I tell you. The gazes of Gabrielle Mina, her fashion of taking my hands and kneading them, so to speak, the kisses on the nape of the neck accompanied by little bites that she soon permitted herself to grant me, and which, out of weakness, I tolerated, and her manner of putting her arm round my waist—yes, by all of that I recognized that she was a lady to be classified solely with ladies . . ."

"But then, what about her adventure, that idyll with Jean des Glaïeuls, the young man of lace and rings, a monsieur to be classified solely with men?"

"Wait . . . that was precisely what excited my curiosity regarding that fake household. They were both admirably bracketed: Mademoiselle Monsieur and Monsieur Mademoiselle. And it's because that idyll in the confines of Mytilene and Sodom captivated me that I scarcely quit its actors. I had complete liberty; the Duc d'Arles had gone to play roulette and my doctor considered me to be cured; I took advantage of that to devote myself entirely to the study of those rare amours, so abnormal in their normality.

"Des Glaïeuls and La Mina now spent all their days with me; we roamed the suburbs in the afternoon. Oh, the landscapes of rubble, the clouds of stinking smoke that made the sky sick and the trees consumptive, those landscapes of desolation that I abominate, and that Jean des Glaïeuls enabled me to love for six months! And when it was not the suburbs, it was little exhibitions of art, paintings, sculptures and jewels; afterwards, we dined on the boulevards, des Italiens or de La Villette, in restaurants frequented by livestock dealers. At nine o'clock, when Gabrielle Mina leapt into a carriage and went to play her role of a gypsy in *Fleurs de trimard*, Jean des Glaïeuls and I wandered, and we met up with the little debutante at midnight, when she came out of the theater . . ."

"And then?"

"Then we went back to my place."

"Your house?"

"Precisely," said Nine. "My house. I offered the couple hospitality every evening. What is more natural? Thus, I had my phenomena always to hand. I could study them and analyze them at close range, at any hour of the day and the night . . ."

I interrupted again.

"You said '*and* the night.' That leads me to think . . ."

I must have had a very equivocal smile, for Nine d'Aubusson replied swiftly: "Don't worry. They didn't sleep in my room and in my bed, but alongside."

"Alongside your bed?"

"Don't be vaudevillesque, my dear Fabrice. You understood perfectly well that des Glaïeuls and Mina slept in an adjacent room. And in order not to have to fear any nocturnal invasion, be persuaded that I locked myself in with a double turn . . . and also shot the bolt."

"That was sage, for with such guests, of such contestable morality, there was everything to fear . . . especially from Gabrielle Mina."

"It was indeed because of her that I took all my precautions. As regards Jean des Glaïeuls, I had no fear, habituated as I was to considering him almost . . . fraternally."

"But brothers have been known . . ."

"You're rambling, my dear."

That was pronounced in a slightly dry tone. Fortunately, a smile arrived almost immediately to correct that moment of ill-humor.

"Yes," Nine went on, "we lived together continuously, therefore, and gradually, I perceived the causes of that liaison; I rationalized it. What each of those two beings loved in the other was their perversity. They esteemed one another for their abnormal aspects; except with the nuance, on the part of Gabrielle Mina, that the esteem was lined with a certain scorn for des Glaïeuls—the scorn of all people who only know of human beings their debauchery and their money.

"As for Jean des Glaïeuls, he was full of petty concerns for his companion. Word of honor, I no longer recognized him; he now had a gallantry, bringing bags of bonbons, carrying umbrellas and abandoning the best seats in carriages. One day, when we had all been out shopping, the fiacre was encumbered by packages that I did not want to be lodged in the carriage, and des Glaïeuls even offered to sit beside the coachman . . . precisely, my dear, beside the coachman!"

"Well, if the coachman was handsome and to his liking," I sniggered, "perhaps our friend was quite satisfied."

"Never in this life . . . a frightful Auvergnat coachman, ignobly bearded. The horror! Anyway, Jean des Glaïeuls didn't climb up on the seat. I opposed it, and on my insistence, he took another carriage, which followed ours. But all alone, he gave the impression of getting bored, poor thing! That was amusing, very amusing.

"So, it was true, then. The ex-overly pretty young man was amorous—amorous! All that there is of the most 1830—and amorous of that little whore!

"But where did it commence and where did it stop, that amour—or rather those amours—of inverts? That was what I was eager to know. How was the rite, the act of union, accomplished? Was it . . . normal, or did it throw the two lovers into the sin of Fraud?

"All those nagging questions were presented to my mind and irritated me more every day. For I still sensed a mystery hiding behind that passion, something monstrously amoral in that idyll. My thought could not admit that Jean des Glaïeuls loved a woman in the manner common to all men. Yes, there was something, a secret . . .

"Merely by the fashion in which the couple kissed one another at my table, before my eyes . . . It was not the true kiss of healthy amour, the rapprochement of two mouths, one offered and the other taking . . . or rather, it was that, but inverted . . .

"Exactly! I gradually had the conviction of it: yes, gradually that idea was imposed on me: Gabrielle

Mina was not Jean des Glaïeuls' mistress, as the latter had told me. She was his lover!

"A crazy idea, an absurd, unreasonable idea, a hypothesis outside all amorous and sexual givens.

"An unexpected encounter in the streets of Paris was soon to give me the key to the mystery, as the late Xavier de Montépin would have said."[1]

---

1 The reference is to the prolific feuilletoniste Xavier de Montépin (1823-1902).

PREDICTION
(*Le Supplement,* 11 April 1903)

"AND that encounter?"

"We're getting to it. We had agreed that each of us would be free that afternoon, so, after lunch, the amorous couple had departed at hazard 'to watch life passing by,' as Jean des Glaïeuls said, and a few minutes later I set forth for the Rue Tronchet, to an exhibition of modern art, where an admirable collection of modern-style jewelry had attracted my attention a few days before."

"Modern-style jewelry!" I had not been able to help exclaiming. "But that's a folly on your part, the modern style. Do you find that epoch so scantly distant—since it's a matter of last year—that you haven't had enough of it?"

"If you keep interrupting me," said Nine d'Aubusson, "the entire night will go by before you've heard the end of my story. And as for resuming it the next night, don't count on me, my dear Fabrice. My name isn't Scheherazade."

"You're much too young, my dear."

Disarmed by that compliment—it really was a compliment—Nine d'Aubusson smiled, and went on:

"So I went to the Modern Art, attracted by the art jewelry on display, the art jewelry of Charles de Monvel.[1] Although you often mock the modern style, I hope that the works of Monvel, like those of Lalique and a few others will find grace in your eyes, but above all Charles de Monvel's. So many charming and bewitching rings, so delicately wrought, pendants, necklaces and brooches, with new harmonious lines, so savant in their sometimes apparent simplicity.

"Charles de Monvel! He's the decorator of women *par excellence*, if I dare put it like that. No one knows better than him how to dispose gems, how to frame them in green gold or old silver, to profuse jewels with rare enamels and opals, chrysoliths and emeralds, pears and pale sapphires-and arrive thus at luminous harmonies, sparkling ensembles, for the sensuality of the eye! The interpretation of insects in modern jewelry is his work. Some rings—that red spider, for instance, which you never take off, is really the most bizarre ring, the strangest that we have seen for a long time . . ."

"My dear friend, if you're beginning to advertise my rings, you haven't finished . . ."

"Don't interrupt me! The jewels of Charles de Monvel recall the Roman or Byzantine orgy,

1 Charles Boutet de Monvel (1855-1913), a notable fabricator of art nouveau jewelry, has a similarly enthusiastic write-up in *L'Araignée rouge*: the ring attributed to him that gave the play and novel of that title their label, and which the narrator of the present story is said to wear, is fictitious.

Heliogabalus or the Paleologues. They're sumptuous, of a slightly sad sumptuousness, which depraves, a sumptuousness that impels to culpable desires . . ."

"So culpable!"

"As you say. So, I was going to admire Monvel's rings, two above all that had conquered me, one adorned by an opal enclosed by two eagle's claws, the other showing a green profile similar to some cameo originating from Memphis. And there, near the carriages, I rediscovered, by the greatest of hazards, a friend—when I say a friend, it's a manner of speaking—the Marquise de Timtubello, an authentic marquise and three times a millionaire for two years, the Timtubello that I had known in my childhood, a dancer under the name of Odette de Lantomne, at the Olympe-Plastique, and even at the Divais Japonen at times of breakdown.

"Today, La Timtubello, approaching fifty, has abandoned herself to Art, with a capital A. Of those old acquaintances she scarcely sees any but demoiselles who throw a footbridge between gallantry and Art, more and more with a capital A. Not young, the lady is rife in the Laffitte and Madeleine quarters, completing by dint of contemplating the Vaseline portraits of Lefèvre, the cold-cream Cupids or Bouguereau tresses passed through oxygenated water of Henner, her science of make-up.[1] She could put on an honor-

---

1 The references are to the portraitists Robert Lefèvre (1755-1830) and Jean-Jacques Henner (1829-1905) and to the style of the prolific William-Adophe Bouguereau (1825-1905).

able show at present of the Princesse de Cadignan of Balzacian memory.[1] You can see that, for an old lady, Art is always useful for something!

"That day, La Timtubello was alone—a rarity! She had disdained her court, her little escort of the young Dispirited—a band of petty messieurs clad in velvet or women's fabrics, Rubemprés, poets or painters in quest of Coralies, Esthers or even Trompe-la-Mort.[2] The guard of honor was only to join her an hour later at the Galerie Georges Petit, where there was a private view of one of those delightful exhibitions of crazy paintings, baroque sculptures and insexual jewels, the annoying tail-end of the artistic movement that you've been defending so vehemently for ten years.

"We were chatting, therefore, with before us, at our feet, a 'charge' of my person by Henry Somm,[3] which I had just discovered, an exceedingly amusing 'charge' at which I was the first to laugh.

"'There's also another of you, which might amuse you less to look at,' La Timtubello assured me, who was continually looking at her finger after smoothing

---

1 The reference is to the heroine of "Une Princesse parisienne" (1833 as a feuilleton in *La Presse*, reprinted in *La Comédie humaine* as *Les Secrets de la princesse de Cadignan*), an early study of an avid and deceptive courtesan.

2 Rubempré and Coralie are characters in Balzac's portmanteau novel *Illusions perdues*, (1837-1843) and Esther a character in its sequel, *Splendeurs et misères des courtisanes* (1838-47); Trompe-la-Mort is a character in Arsène Houssaye's *Madame de Favières* (1844).

3 "Henry Somm" was the pseudonym of the painter and caricaturist François-Clément Sommier (1844-1907).

her hair, doubtless to reassure herself that the dye was still holding.

"'Get away! All charges amuse me.'

"'All?'

"'Indeed. I only ask one thing of them, which is to be witty. If they are, I'm the first to laugh at them . . . and to buy them.'

"'Yes, I understand,' continued the marquise, 'but when they're aggressive . . .'

"'I repeat: if they're witty . . .'

"'. . . Aggressive from the moral viewpoint,' the old lady continued, with a slightly pinched smile. 'You understand, my dear friend, *from the moral viewpoint.*'

"'What does morality have to do with all this?' I couldn't help exclaiming. And in a lower voice, I added: 'Come on, what are you trying to say with your *moral viewpoint,* when it's a matter of an actress, my dear Odette?' I went as far as to use her former forename. 'Evidently, my life has nothing very *moral,* in the bourgeois sense of the word,' I continued, 'but, my dear, let me tell you that it isn't your prerogative to criticize my conduct . . . in fact, you less than anyone else.'

"As you can see, I was piqued. Also, well, she irritated me, that former libidinous woman, with her new pretention to morality. She was forgetting her past too much. I had to rub her nose in it, didn't I?

"She scarcely had a flash of ill-humor in her once-mauve eyes, now wine-lees, and she replied in a honey-eyed voice: 'How you take what I say amiss, my dear child! But if I mention a very compromising charge of you, it's because I have your interest at heart. You interest me greatly . . . yes, truly . . . Listen to me carefully, child. If you're represented lifting a leg in the air before an audience of boors, dancing a frenetic cake-walk on a table in the Café de Paris, perched on smart shoulders on returning from Longchamp, or laying bets at a trente-et-quarante table, all that is part of the advertising of a pretty girl and an actress. All that will always be found very droll, very Parisian. Even if you're caricatured in the arms of an Apache from Montmartre or the river-bank—as was done in the course of your history with that mariner from Boulogne—everyone will laugh, and celebrate you even more . . .

"'But if you allow yourself to be exhibited with a stripper, vaguely theatrical, of the lowest category, and a monsieur universally reputed for his bizarre mores, and whose vice is only pardoned because he writes interesting books and plays, be assured, my girl, that yesterday's laughter will flee you rapidly. Paris, the worldly, artistic, literary, theatrical, boulevardier life—call it what you like—is only interested in the deeds and actions of people until the moment there's a scandal. One can do anything, love anyone, commit any sin, but it mustn't be advertised. In Paris, scandal kills its woman or its man with as much promptitude and as surely as your little d'Arles can hit the bull's-eye at thirty paces.

"'Now, your *charge* in the arms of those two in-dividuals constitutes a scandal, and a big scandal, which you can't resist. The display of that *ménage à trois*, your conversion to the sapphic cult, that Lesbian naturalization, the publicizing of that . . . what is she calling herself now? . . . that Gabrielle Mina, aggravated by Jean-des-Glaïeuls-of-the-lacy-chemises, as one chronicler mocked recently, is a scandal, a scandal that will stir up your enemies, and even your friends. You have your jealousies; who doesn't have their own? Be careful!

"'From one day to the next you risk finding yourself abandoned, with no hope of finding aid and protection; from one day to the next Paris might no longer know you, and no longer want to know you. Your name will be more forgotten than those of cemeteries. You'll be in the position of that poor Honorée Harley, the great mime, the only mime of our epoch, as Séverin is the only mime, poor Honorée Harley, whom Paris has forgotten, whom Paris is allowing to die of starvation, so to speak, on a fifth floor in the Rue Mauberge, because fifteen years ago she forgot that she was a woman and did not have the right to say, out loud, in the middle of a boulevard restaurant, speaking of Sophie Delagrange of the Opéra-Comique: *Keep that table for me and my mistress!*

"'Yes, my child, men will drop you, for if some of them affect to find lesbianism an elegant vice, for which they have all sorts of indulgence, don't forget that it's a long way from theory to practice. A serious lover, an enduring lover, will never take an equivocal mistress. She will only ever appear to him to be possible . . . for others! As for women, the fear of being dropped by their lovers will soon make them desert you, and you'll remain alone with your dishonor . . . be careful! In spite of the hostility of your remarks in my regard, I want, I must, cry to you: *Beware!* Never permit anyone to exhibit you like this again . . .'

"And La Timtubello unfurled before me a caricature representing me caressing the rump of Gabrielle Mina under the eyes of Jean des Glaüieuls, coiffed in a conical cap. 'I bought this petty infamy jut now,' the ex-beauty concluded, 'and I wanted to send it to you as a *Mene, Tekel, Upharsin!* Here it is. And with that,' she concluded, 'permit me to take my leave, for I'm expected at Georges Petit's.'

"And with a very amicable and polite salute, with a hint of irony, and also of tenderness, in her gaze, La Timtubello slipped away, leaving me utterly astounded by her singular prediction."

THE MATELOT REAPPEARS
(*Le Supplement*, 18 April 1903)

"NOT badly reasoned at all, my dear Nine, the advice of your Comtesse Timtubelli . . ."

"Yes, wasn't it? And that's why I was so troubled by it. Ah, the former dancer at the Olympe-Plastique knew society, and men . . . she'd seen so much of them! Certainly, a practical guide for the Parisian courtesan-actress by the Comtesse de Timtubelli would obtain a great success among debutantes, and even the chevronned . . ."

"You're right; that book of advice is lacking. Why hasn't your friend written it? The *Maximes* of the Rue de La Rochefoucauld or the *Caractères* of the Rue de La Bruyère, eh? That's a title, and the only title appropriate to . . ."

"Whatever—and to get back to my story, I've told you that La Timtubelli's warnings had troubled me . . . troubled me greatly, in fact. And I was very pensive when I emerged from the Art Moderne, after having acquired the two rings by Charles de Monvel that I had chosen, very pensive as I walked along the Rue Tronchet and gained the Rue du Havre.

"It's necessary for you to imagine how terrible it is for us—artistes and women—that threat of abandonment, what an inferno opens at our feet when we glimpse the moment when success and the vogue quit us, the Caprice that installs you as queen of Paris and the Fête one day and slyly disembarks you the next in mid-happiness, mid-felicity and mid-glory. In vain one clings hard, in vain one tries to bring back the Caprice; it has fled forever . . . forever, you understand, forever . . .

"And the unfortunate woman, abandoned like a plaything that has ceased to please, a doll thrown into the basket of neglect, no longer has any but one decision to make: to resign herself, to go and live in one of those villas of Repose that are strung along the highways of France, if she had been far-sighted and has not squandered her money and her life, or, if her fortune has ebbed away during the time of glory, to descend into the Vale of Tears of which Scripture talks, rolling around café-concerts and low dives, at the hazard of the errant life.

"Abruptly, having passed the Printemps in the Rue du Havre, where a tumultuous crowd was circulating, I arrived at Savari's, the patissier's, and my hunger awoke. As bold as a page—one needed to be in order to introduce oneself into that packed shop—I slid as far as the counter and there, in an entourage that smacked somewhat of the bazaar: English and American misses with the sickly complexion of young women intoxicated by bad tea; old ladies in hooded capes and flat hats, chattering like magpies; pretentious and stupid petty bourgeoises; I ordered a *marignan*, which I began to devour avidly.

"And suddenly, amid the confusion of guzzling women and children, I discovered Gabrielle Mina. Exactly: Gabrielle Mina, in a corner of the shop, sitting at a side-table, more Jeanne d'Arc of the fortifs than ever, with her virginal tresses, her angular profile and her street-urchin voice. She was not alone; a man, a matelot—a matelot, you hear—was accompanying her.

"A matelot! He was a rather rude fellow, a thickset, red-haired fellow with a suntanned face illuminated by two gilded eyes. Precisely: gilded eyes, the large eyes of a Hindu idol, which could certainly have embraced a quarter of the horizon; immense eyes, whose singularity attracted immediately, fascinating eyes . . .

"Clad in the official costume of the French military marine, the fellow had pushed his beret backwards, and it composed a sort of nimbus for that arrogant head of a merry-making matelot. In front of him, a number of plates and cakes were stacked, which indicated that the man was certainly not letting himself go hungry! Sitting facing him, her elbows on the table, Gabrielle Mina appeared to be calming her companion down—I say calming, because the matelot appeared to be impatient. From time to time, the smile that illuminated his face was extinguished, like a lamp whose wick had been abruptly lowered, and the mariner then made as if to rise to his feet; one sensed that he was about to leave.

"But with a word, Jean des Glaeuls' lover dissipated the fellow's disquiet—who, the smile reappearing on his face, sat down again and recommenced devouring more cakes, masses of cakes absorbed in two mouthfuls and without the slightest order: babas steeped in rum following coffee éclairs, followed by tartlets, and even slices of plum pudding. It was slightly sickening, all that gluttony on the part of the matelot, who had doubtless never seen such a feast. And that appeared to amuse an infantile gallery that had gradually formed around him.

"From my corner, sheltered behind two ladies who were congratulating one another infinitely, I observed the couple and their performance, the false departures of the man and the retentions of Gabrielle Mina. That performance interested me and intrigued me to the highest degree. What did that little comedy mean? How was it that Jean des Glaïeuls was not there, he who ordinarily, before my eyes, did not quit Gabrielle Mina for a moment? Who was this matelot, abruptly fallen into that already passably abnormal amorous adventure?

"I remembered des Glaïeuls' comedy, the story of the matelot that he had told me in order to deceive me regarding the sentiments that were reigning over his mind; I recalled perfectly what I had hitherto regarded as a made-up story. Was hazard about to reveal to me that a matelot really did figure in that . . . idyll?

"No, that was impossible. I could not have allowed myself to be led astray to that extent; the two accomplices could not have played me thus. Anyway, I had never surprised a single word making allusion to that man, or his very existence. Seeing his stratagem discovered, Jean des Glaïeuls had always imitated the prudent silence of Contrart on the subject of the 'boat' that he had 'floated' momentarily for me.[1] Then again, the matelot that I had before my eyes, the seaman with golden eyes in a rubicund face, bore no resemblance to the other mariner, a gamin with candid eyes, whose photograph my friend had shown me . . .

"So?

"So, I lost myself in conjectures, each crazier, stranger and more absurd than the rest.

"What was that matelot doing with Gabrielle Mina? Was he a lover? No, there was nothing in his gestures and his gaze that denounced a lover. And then Gabrielle had declared to me often enough that she did not like men; if she made an exception for Jean des Glaïeuls it was because the pretty young man was a special being . . .

"Was he a brother, a cousin, a relative? No, for at one moment, a second during which the shop was, if not silent, at least less noisy, I had been able to seize this phrase, uttered by Gabrielle Mina:

"'I can never remember your name . . .'

---

1 The reference to "prudent silence" is to a famous sarcastic compliment addressed posthumously to Valentin Contrart (1603-1675), a founder and the perpetual secretary of the Académie française, who never published any of his abundant observations of his contemporaries during his lifetime.

"He was not a relative, then, nor even someone of long acquaintance. So . . . ?

"That interrogative *so* recurred, still nagging, in my mind; and I found no response to it, no argument in favor of any solution. For a curious woman—which is to say, a woman twice over—you can imagine the torture, can't you?

"Oh, too bad. I was about to present myself to the couple; I was about to interrogate Gabrielle Mina . . . I wanted to know, yes, to know . . . and I was already excusing myself to the complimentary old ladies who were serving me as a screen, when, just at the moment when the mariner, finally stuffed with cakes, weary of waiting in that stifling crowd of women and children, being a man of the open air, was getting up to leave, the stature of Jean des Glaïeuls was framed in the door, his bright felt hat pulled down over his eyes and his hands, overladen that day with opals and amethysts, in a 'cakewalk pose.' He advanced toward the couple and abandoned one of his hands to Gabrielle Mina and the other to the matelot.

"And Gabreille Mina's vicious schoolboy voice, rising by a tone, piped: 'Truly, you owe me a fine candle. What trouble I've had keeping him intact and fresh for you! He wanted all the time to flee to a bistro to sink tafia. For sure you owe me a fine candle!'

"The gazes of the matelot and Jean des Glaïeuls were laughing at one another."

A CORNER OF THE VEIL IS LIFTED
(*Le Supplement*, 25 April 1903)

I was delighted—yes, delighted—by the des Glaïeuls-Mina couple. While I believed those two individuals to be "normal in the abnormal," they had still found a means of refining their unhealthy amours, for the presence of that matelot . . . that opened horizons to me, I can assure you!

At that moment, my screen ladies, having finally finished their litany of reciprocal compliments, decided to get a plate and eat a cake; and for that, they approached the table occupied by Gabrielle Mina and the mariner, for the amorous trio was placed next to a dessert-rack—a sage precaution of La Mina, who was thus able to stuff and keep in place the prey that she destined for our friend.

"I took advantage of that fortunate incident to approach the table in all security. A desire had come to me to listen to what the man of joy said to his lover and her companion, without their being aware of my presence, reserving showing myself until the moment when I judged it opportune.

"I therefore executed the movement, and was adroit enough to succeed in it. I now found myself placed immediately behind the trio, with my back to them. Enveloped in my furs, with a hat that La Mina did not know—or had hardly seen—on my head, I was well-placed to spy (let us not mince words) in all security. Although I could not see the accomplices, at least I could hear them; and I can swear to you that I was all ears!

"Their conversation was pretty, and above all polite; I can answer for that! There was a series of indiscreet and indecent questions relating to the virility of the matelot, revolting words for anyone with a hint of morality. But what point is there in talking about morality when it's a matter of Jean des Glaïeuls? One might as well talk about rope in the home of a hanged man, as someone once said.

"Yes, with the flood-gates open, there was an overflow, a tumultuous tide of obscene interrogations and responses, demands from des Glaïeuls and La Mina—La Mina interested in spite of her sapphic doctrines—and assurances on the part of the mariner that he was *good business*, as more than one woman, and more than one man, could certify. And all of that, on the part of des Glaïeuls, Mina and the man, in coarse phrases, in which the words were crude, but of a crudity of which you can have no idea!

"In the end, Jean des Glaïeuls, satisfied with the responses, gibes, allusions and promises of the matelot Latringlette—the man had spoken his name—sent him away, putting a hundred sous in his hand, and arranging a rendezvous for the same evening.

121

"'You understand,' added Gabrielle Mina. 'At half past midnight, 83 Rue de La Bruyère. You ring, you shout *Mina*, outside the concierge's lodge, and you go up to the third. There you knock on the door to the right, and one of us—my friend or me—will open up to you. Agreed? You've understood fully?'

"'Very well,' the matelot assured her. And after shaking hands with the couple, he left the patisserie, strutting like a sea-wolf, happy with himself.

"Left alone, the two accomplices exchanged their impressions.

"'Well, what do you think?' asked Mina.

"'Not bad,' said des Gaïeuls.

"'In sum, you find him to your taste?'

"'My God, for what I want to do!'

"'Exactly. Say it, does he please you?'

"'I'll tell you that tomorrow morning,' replied Jean des Glaïeuls, putting an end to the conversation. 'Let's go.'

"The couple got up and, having settled the bill, went out in their turn, in the midst of the curiosity and the alarm of the clients, astonished by the display of Jean des Glaïeuls' ringed hands.

"A moment later, I was on the sidewalk too, but I could no longer see the two lovers; they were lost in the crowd.

"What was I to do? Go home? Oh, no! And an idea surfaced in my head. I made the resolution to go and deliver myself to a little personal enquiry—very personal—at 83 Rue de La Bruyère. I leapt into a carriage and in less than a quarter of an hour I was engulfed beneath the vault of a nondescript house, of rather mediocre appearance.

"The concierge's lodge was to the right. I decided to go in, to interrogate the Cerberus, who would surely not hesitate, at the sight and touch of a louis, to surrender all the secrets that I wanted to know, regarding the enigma that I wanted to resolve.

"I made the door of the lodge turn on its hinges and . . . I found myself abruptly in an assembly of a dozen women, ladies of the Fontaine quarter, who were perorating, exchanging confidences, dealing cards and sipping their *vertes*, cigarettes in their lips, around a moustached matron nestled in an armchair with wings, around a widow's fire.

"Imagine my astonishment, my surprise, and my confusion! Where I expected to find an old concierge in tête-à-tête, if I might put it like that, with a cat—the legendary concierge, in short—I found a kind of schoolmistress surrounded by pupils! It's true that I was in the Breda quarter: I should have been prepared for that tableau.

"And all those women, esthetes of Montmartre, maids of all work of the Gare Saint-Lazare, drolesses à la Botticelli—naturally!—all those hungry-bellies-have-no-ears, stray cats of the Rat Mort and other Abbeys of Thelema, all those kids—the majority could not be older than twenty-five—were staring at me in the blink of an eye, undressing me with their gazes, expertly.

"The concierge got up.

"'What do you desire, Madame?' she asked.

"In truth, caught on the hop, unable to improvise a lie, I burned my boats and explained the purpose of my visit: 'You have a tenant here, Mademoiselle Gabrielle Mina, don't you, Madame?'

"At the same time, I slipped the old woman a louis.

"'Gabrielle Mina! Yes, Madame,' the concierge replied, conquered by my liberality. And to make the hostility cease that was legible on all those feminine faces, she added: 'Mesdames, Madame is a friend. One can speak before her. She's one of us!'

"Immediately, on all the faces, hostility was succeeded by an eager amity. Yes, the gazes cleared, the foreheads ceased frowning, smiles flourished on lips—all the lips. That *She's one of us*, pronounced by the matron, was the *Open Sesame* of that abode.

"They hastened around me. One rid me of my furs, 'so that you won't catch cold when you leave,' an armchair was rolled out for me, and I was obliged to sit down; a footstool was slid beneath my feet. The old concierge wanted absolutely to yield her foot-warmer to me. I was surrounded, cajoled and cosseted by all those ladies. There were only smiles of joy around me. I was a friend . . . I was one of them.

"Understanding that that was a unique opportunity for me to obtain intimate information about Genrielle Mina and, on the rebound, about her fantasies with Jean des Glaïeuls, in order to loosen tongues—why does that *loosen tongues* make you smile?—I sent someone to fetch six bottles of champagne.

"Then there was delirium; I became the queen of that little feminine and lesbian society. The tes-

124

timonies of amity were redoubled. I had difficulty avoiding certain overly precise touches, certain lips that sought mine too avidly and too gluttonously. At the same time, compliments and eulogies rained down. All those ladies competed to extol my beauty and my charm. And, one of them having remarked on my astonishing resemblance to Nine d'Aubusson, the star of the Olympe-Plastique (I believe you!) one audacious person went so far as to find me better than the actress! And she added, audaciously, that I had youth on my side, triumphant youth, whereas La d'Aubusson was beginning to fill out, to age terribly! That compliment was mixed with insolence, but what medal does not have its reverse side? Then again, there are no roses without thorns, and honey is sometimes bitter!

"Eventually, the transports and effusions of those ladies calmed down somewhat, and I was then able to get to the subject of my visit. And immediately, information abounded.

"Gabrielle Mina! They certainly knew her! Didn't they just! She occupied a beautiful apartment in the house that she only used for amorous rendezvous— and she had enough amorous rendezvous! All the habituées of the *Scarabée rose* and the *Hanneton tricolor* had passed that way, in that discreet dwelling, a chamber of folly from which gasps of amour rose, the inarticulate cries of slow swoons.

"Oh, all those ladies of the house were also very familiar with Mina's little paradise, the chamber of sensuality in which the actress sang the black mass of amour, her bed serving as an altar.

"But now, the mad escapades and ardors of Mina, her scandalous adventures, which were the talk of the quarter and the society of ladies, had changed character, taken another turn, and that since the appearance at the demoiselle's side of a tall young man, powdered, perfumed and bejeweled like a woman, a b***** (they uttered the word without hesitation) for sure!

"Yes, Mina, in the company of her friend, now had rendezvous in the house with men. And what men! Bulls, veritable Hercules, soldiers, sailors, acrobats and bandits!

"I listened to all those details as one listens to a tale of enchantment, avidly . . ."

TOWARD THE SABBAT!
(*Le Supplement*, 2 May 1903)

"ONE of the ladies in the audience, who had complimented me a little while before and had unleashed the famous homage on the subject of my resemblance to . . . myself, outbid all the rest.

"Rubbing against me like an amorous cat, she lavished the most ludicrous details about the amours of Gabrielle Mina and Jean des Glaïeuls, their rendezvous with all the bruisers who filed through the dwelling. And what a procession! The whole crew of Lyonnais brethren had passed that way, even Rodophe le Boucher, the famous Rodolphe who nevertheless had the reputation of not *marching* . . . And animal-tamers, subordinates of the great menageries, and butchers from La Villette, oxherds in blouses and flat caps, bulky and robust ditch-diggers, cuirassiers in full uniform, and a flood—a veritable flood—of mariners, to make one believe that all the squadrons of France were incessantly sending delegations!

"Yes, all those men, that host of individuals, polluted Gabrielle Mina's couch in the company of Jean des Glaïeuls, and only since the young man had become Gabrielle's friend. What could—what must—be happening in that apartment, where the actors of those amorous follies were always and continually threefold? What scenes of culpable amours, of mad lust, of perverse kisses, must those walls see and hear?

"That thought rendered me utterly feverish—yes, feverish, with a complicated, bizarre fever, cruel and delicious at the same time. I confess that it revolted me and it excited me—precisely: excited me—at the same time!

"Oh, to be mingled with one of those unhealthy adventures, to play a role of . . . spectator in one of those sadistic comedies, to participate in all that pleasure, those unnamable joys, if only with the eyes! That was the desire that rose slowly within me, and infiltrated my thoughts perfidiously, stimulating my nerves. Yes, gradually, that desire was drilled into my head, lighting a fire in my veins . . . I got carried away. I was traveling at full steam, I tell you, on the slope of forbidden lusts . . .

"So, when my complimenter whispered to me: 'If you want to witness one of these sessions, I can enable you to see everything!' it was in a breathless voice that I replied to her: 'Oh, yes! But when?'

"'Whenever you wish.'

"'This evening!'

"'This evening, so be it; they've warned the *prob-logue* that they're coming; be here at eleven o'clock. Above all, not a word to these ladies. Come under the pretext of visiting me. Ask for Mademoiselle Ida."

"'Understood!'

"I wanted to give a pecuniary recognition of that Ida's amicable offer and assistance, but she refused the louis that I tried to slide into her hand.

"'No, no—no money between us.'

"'But in sum . . .'

"'You can embrace me for the trouble.'

"The eyes of the donzelle were raised toward me, eyes that were soft . . . too soft. I understood, and did not want to understand. And without conclusion, without saying yes, I got up and took my leave of all those ladies who, now somewhat lit up by the champagne, perhaps too lit up, were exchanging kisses and the names of birds between them.

"And I left that All-Lesbos of the Breda quarter, escorted out by Mademoiselle Ida, who absolutely wanted to put me in a carriage and who only quit me after a 'Don't forget . . . this evening . . . eleven o'clock . . .'

"The carriage pulled away. Half an hour later I was at home, with a slight headache because of the multiple incidents of the excessively full day: the advice of La Timtubelli; the encounter with the des Gläieuls-Mina couple, aggravated by a matelot, at Savarni's patisserie; the investigation at 83 Rue de La Bruyère . . . How many things can happen in Paris in six hours!

"I dined lightly and alone. All those adventures populated my poor brain, and to crown the ensemble, an abominable vision rose up of scenes of amour, such that they were about to be presented in Gabrielle

Mina's apartment in that almost-brothel in the Rue La Bruyère. And I assure you that the tableau in question, created by my imagination, was not made to calm the fever that was consuming me. No, certainly not!

"Let's see, was I going to go to the rendezvous given to me by Mademoiselle Ida? I murmured 'No!' but I thought 'Yes!' Reason said to me: 'Don't go! Why roll in that mud?' but my senses replied: 'You'll go in order to satisfy us.'

"Satisfy my senses! But how? In what fashion? I knew nothing about it—nothing, I tell you. And yet I hoped . . . for what? Nothing, or rather . . .

"I'm trying, my dear Fabrice, to give you an idea of my anguish, of my 'tumult of souls' as your friends the decadents once wrote. But words are impotent to render it to you, that tumult of the soul, to enable you to feel and understand what rose up within me, the hunger for insane lusts that I had just awakened, and which demanded imperiously to be satisfied, in spite of all reason and all sagacity.

"Oh, one does not brush with impunity the disorders and disequilibrations of amour, no matter how normal and healthy in mind one might be. The research of sensuality, again and always, is like a spoiled fruit placed by mistake in a stainless cargo, which corrupts everything. It's necessary never to play with fire; for two months I had been living the same life, breathing the same air, and sleeping next door to Jean des Glaïeuls and Gabrielle Mina, those two monsters of depravity—the masterpiece of inversion, to employ the expression with which Adhémar Le Menestrier qualified them.

"I had to succumb to the temptation. It was fatal. And I had even arrived at finding rather pretty, in my memory, the eyes of that Ida, who had demanded a kiss as recompense for enabling me to see the orgy projected by the couple, when Jean des Glaïeuls, introduced by the chambermaid, came to find me in the dining room where, at the end of the meal, I was nibbling a ginger tart.

"He smiled and exclaimed: 'Ginger preserve for a lady, alone and sage, whose lover is traveling? That, my dear Nine, is a rather dangerous comestible!'

"'No, I assure you,' I protested.

"'In that case, what do you usually need as an aphrodisiac?' he said. 'Daily doses of cantharides, perhaps?'

"I interrupted his mockery. 'Come a little closer, des Glaïeuls.'

"'There, dear friend,'

"'Closer still.'

"'I told you so—it's the effect of the ginger. Only, you know my principles: don't count on me for . . .'

"'You're mad! If I've made you come closer it's to compliment you . . .'

"'On?'

"'On your fine appearance. Not one wrinkle, your few white hairs carefully hidden, a cravat that illuminates your face for us. My compliments; you're eighteen years old this evening.'

"'Thank you, flatterer. Is that to remind me that I passed thirty yesterday?'

"'I repeat to you that you're eighteen years old this evening.'

"'Well, so much the better,' he declared, with a pirouette. 'There are evenings when one loves to be beautiful, and this is one of them.'

"And with his girlish hands, he shifted the bezel of a ring that was inconveniencing him."

THE FROLEUSE[1]
(*Le Supplement*, 12 May 1903)

"'YOU'RE going to rejoin Gabrielle Mina?' I asked.

"'Of course I'm going to rejoin her,' replied Jean des Glaïeuls, 'as I do every evening. They'll end up no longer seeing anyone but me as the little theater.'

"'Well, aren't you the author?'

"'Certainly, but I swear to you that it's the first time in my life that I've been encountered so much in a house where one of my plays is being performed. Generally, when I come to cast an eye two or three times in a hundred representations, that's all I can do.'

"'Get away!'

"'Word of honor, it's as I say. As much as the writing, and the bringing to the stage of one of my comedies enchants me, charms me and conquers me, as much as I enjoy the labor of rehearsals, the performances before the public leave me indifferent, even enervated.

---

1 Dictionaries generally translate the French term *froleuse* as "coquette," but its meaning—a woman who applies friction—is not intended metaphorically in this instance.

Hearing repeated once again phrases that, by dint of being repeated, have become banal, as threadbare as worn-out shoes, and seeing renewed the gestures so laboriously fixed and settled, is exasperating. Oh, how I understand Sardou who, it's said, never appeared at one of his premières! After the first representation, the charm that seemed to be disengaged from the work vanishes; nothing any longer remains but the memory of sterile hours of combat with the memory of the interpreters, and the irritating remembrance of struggles sustained for the regulation of attitudes . . ."

"'In that case, dear friend, you must suffer beside Gabrielle Mina!'

"'Oh, a little . . . but you know, my dear Nine, I spend my evenings in her dressing-room rather than in the hall.'

"'And after your evening, when you don't come to ask me for hospitality, may I know where you go?'

"That question escaped involuntarily, so to speak, from my lips I couldn't help it. I wanted to know . . . O curiosity!

"'What we do afterwards . . .' replied Jean des Glaïeuls, slightly embarrassed by the brutality of my question, 'my God . . .'

"'Come on, confess . . . I won't eat you, I'm not an ogress. And then, you know full well that I have every indulgence for you. What do you do after the performance? Where do the two of you drag your cravats by night?'

"He had had time to pull himself together, and it was in a detached voice, with a smile flourishing on his mouth, scarcely shaded by a fine moustache raised in feline fashion that he pronounced:

"'Oh, we don't do anything bad, you know, my dear friend. We're very idyllic—too idyllic, even . . . a bavaroise on the boulevard and two hours in a carriage through the solitary paths of the Bois . . .'

"'The Bois, at two o'clock in the morning?'

"'Why not?'

"'In what hope?'

"'What do you mean by hope?'

"'You understand me perfectly well!'

"'On my honor, no.'

"'Well, then, I'll ask the question crudely. Do you wander through the Bois in the hope of provoking an emotion?'

"'My word, no. You know full well that I no longer have any vice.'

"'You have a nerve!'

"'There's no nerve but yours; I no longer have any vice. Gabrielle Mina has brought me back to normal amour.'

"'Repeat that lie again.'

"'But why do you want me to be lying? With what end?'

"'Does one ever know with you?'

"'I'll tell you the same until tomorrow. I'm now converted, and forever. I love women, and I even . . .'

"'Shh!'

"'. . . show them my sentiments, whatever happens. In any case, I don't know where you're trying to go with your strict interrogation. You, more than anyone else, are not unaware of my abjuration of the rites that I celebrate in honor of my contemporaries in the flesh. And now, my dear Nine, let me take my leave of you. Gabrielle expects me at the theater in good time, and I came to warn you that it will doubtless be two or three days before you see us again . . .'

"'Bah! That's an abandonment! Where are you going?'

"'To take advantage of my lover's two days of leave to explore the woods, the woods of Meudon, as the ballads sing . . . I'm shouting in order to reassure you that we're idyllic!'

"With that, he held out his hands to me and disappeared, leaving me astounded by his brazenness in lying.

"There is no need to tell you, is there, that that had decided me? An hour later, in a very simple costume, I had returned to the Rue de La Bruyère, where a number of those rediscovered ladies, returned to 'work,' received me as an old acquaintance with kisses, congratulations, caresses, etc. It was truly embarrassing—very, very embarrassing.

"I enquired about Mademoiselle Ida; she was in the house and she was going to come down; in fact, five minutes later, Mademoiselle Ida appeared in the most Nile-green of the brothel's peignoirs, and threw her arms around me.

Immediately, all those ladies, misunderstanding the nature of our meeting, gave me a little more room.

"'She's chosen Ida,' murmured one of them. 'She doesn't have bad taste!'

"'One little ménage more in the house!' someone replied. 'But Gabrielle Mina will be furious when she finds out that she's been so swiftly replaced.'

"'Bah! It's already two months and a half since Ida and Gabrielle broke up. Gabrielle is reasonable enough to know that a woman isn't made of wood.'

"Ida took me away just as that dialogue concluded, and we went up to her room—which is to say, into an amorous apartment in the furnished house, two rooms, drawing-room and bedroom, plus a toilet cabinet: the eternal lodging of the ladies of the Fontaine quarter. You know those interiors as well, if not better, than me; there's no need to describe it for you.

"As soon as we were in her drawing-room, where a sofa on which I took my place groaned in all its springs—how much service the poor thing must have seen!—I interrogated her regarding the words I had just overheard.

"'Well, yes,' she confessed, 'I'm Gabrielle's former pippin, and it's for that dirty individual with a mouth full of rice powder that she dumped me. And that's why I'll help you to see and do whatever you wish.'

"'To do what?'

"'Oh, so you think I'm stupid? But I've guessed . . . everything. It isn't for Gabrielle that you came here, and that you want to catch them in the act; it's for the mec. A funny idea, to have a yen for such types: girl-men. If one likes girls, like me, at least one takes a woman, a true woman, not a fellow of that type, nei-

137

ther flesh nor fowl, neither man nor woman. In the end, though, amour can't be commanded, can it? And I'd be wasting my time preaching morality to you!'

"'You think, then . . .'

"'That you're hooked on that b***** (she uttered the word unthinkingly). Of course! One can see that, simply by the way that you're occupied with him!'

"'But I swear to you . . .'

"'It's your business; all that I can tell you is that if you need a hand to squash him, I'm yours, for we'd be avenging both of us. And you know that I have the necessary here . . .'

"At the same time she showed me a revolver and a yataghan of respectable dimensions.

"'That'll do the job,' she continued.

"'You're strangely mistaken, Mademoiselle Ida.'

"'Ta ta ta! It's rubbish, all that. You can trust me. I tell you that I understand your sentiments . . . and have no fear; it isn't me who'll ever talk at the station, if we're forced to go there. Affairs of amour, you see, are sacred! I'd rather die than squeal . . .'

"I was literally terrified.

"'Unless,' continued the client of Montnartrean brasseries, in her picturesque and vaguely argotic French, 'you want me to avenge you in another fashion . . .'

"Illuminating me with her eyes, with inviting gestures toward the bed whose curtains were drawn back, she concluded: 'To punish them, we can put horns on both of them . . . what do you think, eh? Do you like the plan?'

"And the singular young woman pressed herself against me, putting an arm around my waist, and her soft, slightly dead, voice murmured: 'It's so good to rub against a pretty woman . . . do you want to?'

"The adventure was becoming singularly complicated. Into what wasps' nest had I recklessly thrown myself?"

THE HOUSE OF A HUNDRED EYES
(*Le Supplement*, 16 May 1903)

AND Nine d'Aubusson continued: "A minute more and I was weakening in the arms of the froleuse, who was gripping my waist and trying to draw me toward the mystery of the alcove. But I stiffened myself and, in spite of my disturbance, found the strength to reckon with the amorous demoiselle.

"'Come on, my dear . . . you can't think so. We hardly know one another, and our acquaintance is so recent. Let's at least wait . . .'

"That *at least wait*, Ida presumably took as an acquiescence to her desires, for she released me, and said: 'You're right,' Then she took her place beside me on the sofa.

"Immediately, I continued to interrogate her. What more did she know about the Gabrielle Mina-Jean des Glaïeuls couple? Could she tell me . . . unusual things, of which I might be unaware? Did she know the precise preliminaries of that union?

"'Do I know them!' the demoiselle exclaimed. 'Certainly. It's in this house that the idyll was sealed, after a rehearsal of *Fleurs de trimard*. Jean des Glaïeuls came back with Gabriele Mina in order to teach her a song that she had to perform in the course of the play. And that argotic song, a true declaration of amour to a runner of the slope and the banks, stimulated Gabrielle's imagination, made her cluck, lit up the flowery agate of her eyes of an amour she-cat.

"'I witnessed that private and intimate rehearsal,' she continued. 'It happened in Mina's room, where a piano had been hired for the purpose. Des Glaïeuls, sitting at the instrument, ran his weary ring-laden fingers over the keys, accompanying the voice of his interpreter, who, leaning over him, was shivering, certainly labored by some insane desire. She sang, entirely given to the crapulous refrain:

I have him in my blood, the man I love!

"'Her voice was so abandoned and so languorous that it attracted Émile: Mimile the house-boy, the guardian of this temple of All-Lesbos, the guardian of the seraglio for ladies only; Mimile, who combines the functions of cleaner, commissionaire and even chauffeur, when the ladies, sufficiently at leisure, depart in a cluster in a limousine to entertain the suburbs with their songs and lewd laughter.

"'Mimile, a former mariner, one-time wrestler and then bodyguard to a young sugar-manufacturer, finally ran aground in the hospitable dwelling of these ladies after a stint behind the counter of a Batignollaise herborist's shop whose tenant had the

141

misfortune of going to Clermont for having sunk and caused to perish a Malthusian client. Mimile: a bandit of all trades, what!

"'His entrance into Mina's room, where she was vibrant with music, caused a sensation. Des Glaïeuls turned round, perceived the man—a strapping fellow whose stature he appreciated at first glance, the powerful nose a promising sign of delights, and asked Gabrielle to introduce him.

"'La Mina obliged immediately, glad to find a pretext to make the young man of joy return to her abode as often as possible. Des Glaïeuls gave Mimile the warmest possible welcome, and slipped him the most compromising of winks, regarding which the former wrestler could not be mistaken—and he certainly wasn't mistaken.

"'Personally,' Ida continued, 'I found that very amusing, and it hardly embarrassed me; it was all the same to me, provided that Gabrielle—my lover—didn't desert me. But that was when things went awry, when I had a presentiment of the separation, the rupture that was about to be produced. When the music lesson finished, des Glaïeuls invited Mina and Mimile to dinner, not even giving me the alms of a glance. Mimile accepted, with the boss's permission, and the trio went off, leaving me alone—without a glance, I repeat!

"'You can guess what followed, can't you? And there's no need to dot the *is* for you. The day after, the young author and Mimile were the best of friends, and Gabrielle Mina presided over their singular betrothal. Gabrielle Mina was promoted to the rank of procuress of des Glaïeuls' pleasure, and dropped me brutally, for no reason . . . and it's since that day that the strange life of the couple commenced, for Mimile, soon fallen into disgrace, was succeeded by the band that has been enumerated to you: soldiers, bandits, pimps . . . what do I know?

"'That didn't always go smoothly, of course. More than once, in the two months that that diabolical existence unfolded, there were squabbles; people brought here caused talk, provoked scandal, and one night, a fortnight ago, the house was woken up by noises, howling like beasts being slaughtered. One of the couple's temporary fancies, unsatisfied with the salary, had attempted blackmail, to extract a little more money by means of threats and then by means of terror. Without the intervention of Mimile, who arrived just in time, things would infallibly have turned out badly; but with Mimile's aid, everything reentered into normality. The sturdy fellow seized the perturbator by the shoulders and made him descend the staircase with kicks, in spite of the cries of the man, who was vomiting vile insults. The day after that affair, Mimile was compensated for the valor of his fists and feet with a signet-ring, of which he was very proud.'

"'But doesn't the landlady protest?' I asked. 'Isn't she afraid of a scandal?'

"'A scandal? You're joking. The house has been well-known for a long time. Many such scenes happen.'

"'Truly?'

"'Positively. And then, des Glaïeuls and Mina have the supreme argument in their favor: money. They give without counting, buying everyone's complaisance and silence, all consciences and all hearts.'

"'Are there really consciences and hearts here?'

"'There's me,' said Ida, grimly. 'Me, who never forgets an insult and disdains money—that money most of all. I haven't forgotten the affront, Gabrielle dumping me, my Gabrielle, of whom I was so fond! And it's since that day that my hatred has grown for that crapulous man, and that's why I'm all yours today—I can't repeat it to you too often—in order to avenge you and avenge myself, no matter by what means.'

"She still had flashing eyes and muted intonations in her voice; but all that dissolved abruptly in a caress for me, an enervatingly passionate caress, an assault, a veritable assault from which I had some difficulty defending myself . . .

"Suddenly, there were noises on the staircase, two human footfalls. Someone was coming up—and I recognized the light—felted, so to speak—tread of des Glaïeuls, mingled with a heavier tread and the clink of a saber against the steps.

"Ida seized my arm. 'It's him, isn't it?' I interrogated.

"'Yes, it's him, the first at the rendezvous.'

"'But he isn't alone. There's a man with him . . .'

"'No change there.'

"'And Gabrielle Mina?'

"'Oh, she won't be here before half past midnight.'

"'But he and she have arranged a rendezvous with a mariner. And that soldier . . . ?'

"'Bah! Do you think that two rendezvous on the same night inconveniences Jean des Glaïeuls?' Ida mocked. She added: 'We're going to watch them!'

"'Really? Without being seen?'

"'Without being seen. You ought to suppose that in a house like this one, everything has been foreseen. The doors hear and the walls have eyes.'

"'Get away!'

"'You're about to be convinced of it. But hush now! Let's climb up on the bed and extinguish the light.'

"I hoisted myself up next to my accomplice and, with the lamp blown out, we waited in silence and darkness. We didn't have to wait long, for the door of Gabrielle Mina's apartment was swiftly opened and then closed again on the passage of two men; a match flared, and the candles of a piano emitted a vague light . . .

"And I saw everything; I saw it through holes cleverly drilled in the wall. I saw and I heard! Oh, that house had a hundred eyes and a hundred ears!

"'And it's like this in all the rooms in the house,' Ida whispered in my ear. 'Oh, the boss is a clever woman and her doss-house is a gold-mine. She has a clientele in all ranks of society, including the proudest . . .'

"I saw, and I heard!

"Having taken off his soft hat, des Glaïeluls aided his companion, a veritable colossus, to rid himself of his cloak, installed him before a small side-table on which he deposited treats, cakes and bonbons, and above all bottles of liquor.

"The guest let him do it, slightly embarrassed by that eager welcome.

"'Doubtless he isn't very accustomed to it,' Ida whispered to me.

"And, in fact, he must not have been very accustomed to it, for Jean des Glaïeuls seemed slightly embarrassed, so embarrassed that he exchanged banal remarks with his partner about rain, good weather and the tribulations and tedium of military life—all of that punctuated with little glasses and cigarettes.

"The man, gradually warmed up, became animated; he was talking about women now; and des Glaïeuls interrogated him regarding his preferences, his tastes and his pleasure. And the other became more and more animated, more and more . . ."

AN EVENING OF POISONS
(*Le Supplement*, 23 May, 1903)

For Mistinguette[1]

"AND the man became more and more lit up . . . "He became so lit up—pardon the bad wordplay—that Jean des Glaïeuls extinguished the candles with a flick of his fan, hiding from our eyes the continuation of that equivocal adventure.

"You can imagine my chagrin, my rage and my rancor at that Robert Houdin trick. For it was a true disappearing act, and I was almost foaming.

"Thinking, sensing, hearing—for they were talking, engaging in a dialogue, the wretches!—knowing that there, scarcely a meter away for us, two beings were communing, two souls flying toward the paradise of

---

1 "Mistinguett" (Jeanne Bourgeois, 1875-1956) was still at the beginning of her career when the present story was written, when she used various renderings of her pseudonym, including the one cited by Fabrice, but she went on to become the most successful cabaret artiste of her era, as well as making numerous movies.

lust, and not being able to mingle with it, to participate, at least fractionally, in that temporary happiness! And from the chamber of pleasure came, in amorous bouquets, exclamations of joy—anticipated exclamations—pleasant surprises, phrases of request and offers.

"I tell you, it was intolerable, for any sensual being.

"Suddenly, after the silence of a well-earned repose, the candle was reilluminated, and its light revealed to me, in the décor of the room, the artilleryman finishing buckling his centurion, doubtless undone by carelessness, and like a mummy sheathed in a strange plush robe, a chrysoprase-green plush punctuated with sulfurous irises, Jean des Glaïeuls, swooning on the ravaged bed, who had profited from the darkness to disguise himself as a priestess of decadent amour.

"With a weary gesture, our friend dismissed the soldier, after having put a louis in his hand, and the man, very sprightly, having surreptitiously collected a pack of cigarettes that was lying around, took his leave, with a mixture of gaucherie and boldness. Five minutes later, his spurred footsteps died away in the depths of the staircase.

"Jean des Glaïeuls! What a derelict, what a human rag, what a ruin! He was still not moving. 'Truly, he hurries his pleasures,' I couldn't help murmuring in my companion's ear.'

"'Oh, yes, he's very quick!'

"'So I've perceived. One could almost believe that he's paid for the room!'

"'And yet he gives thirteen to the dozen. And don't forget that in the house, all the ladies say that he has the soul of a riverside whore of the bank . . .'

"'A riverside whore, a lover of the banks. I've known that for a long time. But shh! He's moving.'

"Monsieur Messaline stretched himself, reached nonchalantly for a blond and silver box on the nearby nightstand, seized a minuscule golden Pravaz syringe, and with the same nonchalance, charged it with the liquid poison that we all know, and know too well: morphine.

"Briskly, he pricked his arm.

"Again there were footsteps on the staircase, a rap on the door, an 'Enter!' launched from the tips of the lips, and there was the irruption of the matelot Latringlette into that equivocal brothel.

"And you can imagine from here the appearance of that Latringlette, a mariner on leave in Paris. He was in a more-than-joyful state. Think of the number of little glasses represented by a hundred sous! A blissful smile illuminated his tanned face, and it was in a merry voice that he enquired: 'Well, sailor, are you in a flat calm? You're out of breath, then. Or has there been too much wind in your sails?' And Latringlette laughed at his joke.

"Des Glaïeuls did not say a word.

"Latringlette enquired, this time in an anxious voice: 'It's not on, then?'

"He approached his big benevolent head to Jean des Glaïeuls' bloodless face, in which, under the skin, of a lily-and-rose complexion, the skull, the hideous death's-head, seemed to be visible.

"Jean des Glaïeuls raised a dead eyelid and in a dying voice, he murmured: 'Remain tranquil for a few minutes. I'm frightfully tired. There are liqueurs on the side-table. Take whatever you wish.'

"And, rolled up in his disconcerting robe, he turned his face toward the wall, after a dolorous stretch that caused his bones to crack.

"Without saying yes or no, his gait unsteady, the matelot headed for the side-table, seized the bottles, uncorked them, sniffed them and put them down again, grimacing.

"'Syrups,' he muttered, 'nothing but syrups, or dirty tafia, overly mild alcohol, which is poison, damn it. And what's this?'

"He picked up a large pharmacy bottle and removed the stopper. 'Ether!' he exclaimed.

"In fact, a strong odor of ether spread through the room.

"He continued, sniffing the neck of the bottle: "Ether! At least that's nice!' And between two respirations, addressing Jean des Glaïeuls: 'Would it bother you if I took a little; it would give me pleasure.' His voice had changed again, becoming suppliant and infantile. And as Jean des Glaïeuls did not reply he went on: 'It's because, you know—or you don't know—of all the memories that ether brings back to me. I took so much in the hospital . . . in China . . .'

"He let himself fall into an armchair, poured a strong dose of the crystalline poison into a glass and drank it abruptly, gluttonously, without a muscle in his face quivering; the man's stomach was evidently habituated to the worst alcohols.

"In five minutes—five long minutes, five centuries—a silence only broken by the buzzing of a fly reigned in the room, that chamber of lust, folly and death, the chamber where, on the one hand, Jean des Glaïeuls, floating in the blue infernos of morphine, was displaying his rigid person on a banal hotel bed, and on the other hand, the matelot, that Latringlette, the uncertain acquaintance of a few hours, was sprawling his drunken body in an armchair.

"It was terrifying! It had all the appearances, all the exteriority, of a tale by Edgar Poe or a poem by Baudelaire; yes, in truth, it was lugubrious—and grotesque!

"The matelot was rambling now, speaking aloud, memories scattered like straw traversing his thoughts and escaping from his lips, visions resurfacing in that memory of a naïve soul, so close to nature. They were of lands traversed and glimpsed during two years of navigation, all his amorous adventures, even of forbidden amours, the evocation of so many lips kissed, so many furtive and sinful embraces harvested at hazard on roads and in ports, so many brief possessions, lascivious or sanguinary, so much Amour, so much Joy collected in all climes and under all latitudes, in the India of millenary legend, floral Japan and brutal North America. Yes, from the open floodgates an entire past surged forth, resuscitated, of the pleasures of the Kiss under unknown skies, in all the ports of the world, or beneath the superb crosses of masts and yardarms.

"And the matelot talked, he confessed, he narrated his life story, his good fortunes of old, mingled with his hopes for the future; he struggled against the Destiny that retained him on *terra firma*; he wept, laughed, cried out . . ."

A NOSTALGIC SOUL
(*Le Supplement*, 30 May 1903)

"OH, the intoxication of that matelot, the intoxication of the Latringlette, can you imagine it? Can you see him writhing, appealing, howling, prey to a crisis of ether, his soul departed toward the white regions of artificial paradises?

"How he was suffering, the poor fellow, how he was bellowing his suffering, his need for the beyond and the dream, the need that claws seamen so forcefully who have savored voyages and whom life retains on land; how all his memories of good roaming in all the continents of the world were torturing him!

"Now, there was always Amour, in all the landscapes resuscitated by his imagination in the course of that crisis, always Eros, the conquering god who appears, Eros, King of the World and almost sole Master of Destiny. There was Amour in its most vibrant formula of lust, Amour that engenders assassination or violation, Amour in blood and in tears, adventurous Amour, truly adventurous, in sum; that was the

Amour that sang on the lips of that naïve brute made of simple instinctive desires.

"It filed past as if in a phonograph, that incoherent confession of so many evenings of revelry, so many nights of pleasure lived in the low streets of the ports of all continents: Marseille, Singapore, Yokohama and New York; and it always dressed a unique altar to the monster, to the ghoul of the hot streets, the eternal whore, the bitter merchant of hopes and appeasement, the sinister vampire of hearts and *écus*, the seducer of matelots offered to the appetite of all those males in rut.

"And it was her, it was the hideous ghoul, that he always summoned, incessantly; it was toward her, toward that phantom reminiscent of a hydra of flame with renascent heads, that he extended his pithy arms. It was as if he had a trepanation of the frontal bone of the skull, and his temples seemed to him to be horns over ardent brands. A diabolical and subtle spirit breathed terrible suggestions in his ear, which were unleashed like a tempest under his cranium and shook the edifice of his being almost in its foundations.

"Sweat inundated his face in the course of that battle with memory. How he must have been suffering from that mad, absurd conflict, that relentless struggle against the Phantom of the Past, the luminous nightmare that was martyrizing his torpid intelligence. Voices were howling; the voices of the awakened ghoul whispering in his ear, and the wings of night-birds were battering his forehead!

"And then, gradually, from that chaos, that terrifying medley of evocation, a figure appeared in the foreground, became detached, isolated, and absorbed all interest around it. And Latringlette's nightmare turned to the amiable. It no longer made his teeth grind, no longer tortured the poor fellow.

"Yes, the wretched etheromaniac was no longer howling mortally. On the contrary; after a few minutes of silence his facial features passed from terror to repose, and then to a mild joy. The laughing, wide open eyes smiled, as if at an agreeable and calming vision. A happy serenity settled over that poor brain sick with poison.

"Words, shreds of phrases, which I pieced together slowly, initiated me to that lust. A name was whispered, a name that returned incessantly and which, in the mouth of the matelot, had a singular, troubling softness: Yacca . . .

"Yacca, a frail and slender mousmé with nacreous skin and gracile limbs; Yacca, doubtless some Japanese custodian of a flower-boat, whom I imagined in a robe with pagoda sleeves, with long pins plunged in her hair, carefully pulled and smoothed; Yacca, doubtless similar to the individuals who populate bazaar screens.

"And Latringlette was singing now, his voice distant, as if heard from the Beyond:

In a white palace of Yeddo
The young empress was dying,
Because, one evening, on the water's edge
A chrysanthemum had her caprice . . .

"Latringlette sang, and sang . . .

"And that voice of the Beyond and the distance, sang all the incurable melancholy of the Breton soul, the soul nostalgic for *Elsewhere*; the Armorican soul and its very special poetry, alternately noted, like a page of sheet music, in major and minor keys, especially the minor . . . It sang, that voice, the distress of those gray souls who suffer in the sunlight, only loving half-tones and taking alarm, jibbing before fanfares of color; it sang, that voice, the great, immense sadness of Bretagne and Bretons before everything that is not their homeland; it explained, that voice, the mortal ennui of lads departed through the World, and their alcoholism under all latitudes, the alcoholism to forget the present and see into the past . . .

> *Soul of the mariner,*
> *Soul of chagrin . . .*

"And it was all that flowing away, all that despair, that was in the depths of Latringlette's divagations, in the depths of his songs . . .

"Jean des Glaïeuls, sprawled on the hotel bed, had changed his position now. He was lying on his back, increasingly reminiscent of a disquieting divinity with his green robe flowery with sulfurous irises and his mask of death and madness, and in a glare of white enamel, the orbs of his revulsed eyes gleamed.

"Oh, the frightful vision, the nightmare vision of those two individuals drunk on ether and morphine!

If I live to be a hundred I shall never be able to erase that vision from my memory!

Latringlette, entirely given to the joy of an interior felicity, his thought departed toward Yacca, the slender Nipponese doll, and Japan, had fallen silent; only the panting respiration of Jean des Glaïeuls whistled in the darkness, a respiration mingled with gasps, the terrible gasps of opium slumber. And it was terrible, that silence, only troubled by those agonized sighs. It hallucinated me in its turn, to the point of crying out.

"Yes, in truth, I was afraid of everything and of nothing: of the sleepers in the next room, of Ida, my companion, of myself. It seemed to me that I had suddenly fallen into the Dantesque circles, that I had just mingled with some terrible imaginary procession painted by Henry de Groux.[1] My pulse accelerated; a fever rose within me, my sang-froid capsized . . .

"Her! Her! My sick brain beat the country; I suffered all the panic of the infernos of lust, those infernos so close at hand, so adjacent to those of Terror. I wanted to leap down from the bed from which I was observing that scene, I wanted to irrupt into the chamber of torturing pleasures where the two men were savoring such strange joys, and snatch them from their madness, whatever the cost . . . And I was going to hammer on the door, with blows of my firsts and fingernails . . .

---

1 The Belgian Symbolist Henry de Groux (1866-1930) was at the heart of the Decadent Movement after moving to Paris; his Bohemian lifestyle, reflected in the hectic violence of many of his paintings, made Jean Lorrain's affectations seem tame.

But Ida was there, beside me: Ida, who sensed my desire and did not want it to be realized; Ida, who retained me, chaining me to her side by means of a: 'Don't move!'

"'But they're killing themselves!'

"'No, they're brutalizing themselves.'

"'It's necessary to save them, Ida!'

"'Why? Anyway, they aren't in danger. Des Glaïeuls is an inveterate morphinomaniac, on whom the poison always acts in this way. It isn't the first time that I've observed that swine pricking himself with his filth. It appears that it gets Monsieur ready—or, rather, Mademoiselle. Isn't it sickening to see that? As for the matelot, he's drunk, that's all, drunk on ether as he would be drunk on rum. But truly, what he spouts of chaplets of bells and drinking songs! That's a client whom ether tenderizes!'

"And she uttered the silent laughter of a civil servant. Then she continued: 'Let's leave those two calves to take care of themselves, then. They'll wake up by themselves without us. Then again, Mina won't take long to appear, and that will be amusing.'

"'Mina! That's true; I'd completely forgotten her.'

"'Ah! Well, you can be sure that she won't forget. And if you've never witnessed a session of wild beasts, you can regale yourself . . . and royally!'

"'What do you mean?'

"'Nothing. I'm keeping the surprise for you. You'll see.'

"'But in sum . . .'

"'I don't let go of anything. Anyway, enough talk about those camels! Let's pay attention to ourselves. It's high time, eh, my darling!'

"Again, Ida enlaced me tenderly, impetuously, and kissed me swiftly, biting my neck.

"What was I to do? What could I do?

"I struggled; I resisted; we wrestled, silently, or, rather teased one another, and gradually, under the intoxication of those savant and so expertly straying caresses, my resistance softened, little by little . . . and Ida made me slide into her arms . . ."

AFTER THE SIN
(*Le Supplement*, 6 June 1903)

I heard, tiron fa la lir lira,
I heard all the fine sailors sing,
All the fine sailors sing la lire
All the fine sailors sing . . .

"IT was the voice of Latringlette, coming from the room next door, a veiled voice of a man drunk on ether, a voice as if dragged through the gutter, public meetings or formidable pub-crawls, the voice of a matelot howling a Breton song, which woke me from my torpor, from my sweet sensual slumber in Ida's arms.

"In Ida's arms! I had arrived—I, Nine d'Aubusson—at letting myself yield to Sin in the embrace of a peripatician of the bitumen, a whore of the lowest class, almost a streetwalker, a demoiselle at ten francs a go; I, Nine d'Aubusson, who had previously rejected the most flattering, the most eloquent invitations to the voyage to Mytilene from more than one authentic and beautiful woman of the world, who had had the courage—a courage that could even be qualified as cruelty—to refuse the flowers and presents of the Marquise de Tramontaine, the adorable Italienne who had been nicknamed the Marquise de Sade, exactly like the heroine of Rachilde's marvelous novel; I, Nine d'Aubusson . . .

"I could not believe the reality. This was where my insatiable curiosity regarding the vices of Jean des Glaïeuls, my desire, my need to know, to see one of his sessions of forbidden amour, had led me! Horror! I had become a lesbian—me! Me, a pervert, an abnormal being!

"Yes. I now had the sentiment that it is dangerous to play with fire, that it is imprudent to skirt precipices, because fire and the abyss attract irresistibly!

Sire le Duc, tiron fa la lir li lira,
Sire le Duc, give me your daughter,
Give me your daughter, la lira.
Give me your daughter.

Poor sinner, tiron fa la lir li lira.
Poor sinner, you're not rich enough,
You're not rich enough, la lira,
You're not rich enough.

"Latringlette continued his song. It was the only sound that was coming from the room next door. Jean des Glaïeuls must still have been asleep, annihilated in his morphine dream, a dream that must not have been interrupted, unless . . . yes, unless, during my somnolence, things had happened . . .

161

"For, how long had I been there, lying in Ida's arms, my body weary, my head fatigued, my mouth dry, not speaking, nor sighing, utterly languid next to my companion of the moment, who was also asleep, as exhausted as me, if not more so, not even troubled by Latringlette's voice? Had it been for minutes or for hours that I had been dreaming, half-asleep, in the black cradling silence in which everything died, and in which I felt myself dying too? Minutes or hours? Honestly, with my head on the block, I would not have been able to answer.

I have more wealth, tiron fa la lir li lira,
I have more wealth than the Duc and his daughter.
Than the Duc and his daughter, la lira
Than the Duc and his daughter.

I have three boats, tiron far la lir li lira,
I have three boats that sail on the sea,
That sail on the sea, a lire,
That sail on the sea.

"'Shut up!' ordered a woman's voice. 'You'll make the whole house howl!'

"Immediately, I was entirely awake, and I sat up abruptly on the bed. I had just recognized the voice of Gabrielle Mina.

"Yes, the voice of Gabrielle Mina, the voice that I would have recognized among a thousand, among ten thousand!

"She was there, that Gabrielle, next door; she had arrived and I had not heard her come in. Decidedly, it was necessary to agree, I had been asleep for hours, exhausted by a sensuality new for me, and also, perhaps, by the reek of ether that traversed the partition wall.

"I had fallen asleep—which is to say that I had certainly spoiled the vision for which I had thrown myself into that equivocal adventure. I had fallen asleep! And it was Ida that I held responsible for that failure, poor Ida, who, awakened by my somersaults on the bed, was rubbing against me, recommencing—or trying to recommence—the irritating game of the froleuse.

"'No!' I shoved her away, swiftly and rudely.

"In spite of her habitude of arguments, the Montmartrean merchant of amour was utterly nonplussed, and it was with the timidity of a schoolgirl, the gaucherie of a little girl caught at fault, that she asked me, naively: 'You don't love me any more, then?'

"I didn't love her any more! A disconcerting question! But in order not to love her any more, it would have been necessary for me to have loved her first, that girl I had not known six hours before my . . . fall, into her arms!

"So much candor and abandonment, that sadness of a beaten dog divined, disarmed me. Truly, it would have been too cruel to be ironic at that moment in response to the poor thing, for whom amour had not grown in my heart with the rapidity of mushrooms in damp weather.

"I preferred to reply: 'But yes, Ida. I have a great deal of sympathy for you'—a phrase that did not engage me excessively. And then, I repeat, why cause chagrin to a young person whom I did not expect ever to see again? It would have been truly inhuman, wouldn't it?

"Slightly reassured, she continued: 'Have I given you . . . pleasure?'

"'Yes.'

"'A lot of pleasure?'

"'Yes, I assure you, Ida."

"'Why are you saying *vous* to me, then? Say *tu!*"

"'It's just . . .'

"'What?'

"'I don't really like saying *tu* . . . I find it a trifle . . . vulgar.'

"'Yes, but between us . . . it's not the same thing. If you knew how good it would seem to me if you say *tu* to me . . . Go on, say *tu!*'

"'Well, if you wish . . . are you content?"

"'Oh, yes, darling!'

"With that, in order to punctuate that conversation in a low voice and to mark her satisfaction, she kissed me gluttonously, with passion. And before I had time to collect myself, still in a low voice, she gave me an account of the emptiness of her life, the Sahara of her affections . . .

"Love a man? But until now, she had known nothing in men but the gross and harsh desire of the client, all the ignominy of the male who pays and only considers a woman as a beast of lust, pleasurable flesh that ought to yield to all demands and all caprices; the wretch, usually drunk, who wants it all for his money, his half-louis, when it is not a hundred sous, or less, a less sometimes further corroded by 'discount.' Her first lover? A vague dauber of the Butte, who had made her leave the studio of couture and her family in order to dump her fifteen months later, without a sou, without a domicile and with a kid. The miserable, banal and frequent story of seduced women.

"Her second lover? Even worse than the first, an ignoble pimp who had picked her up, clothed her, and sent her out to the boulevards, a pimp of whom she had had the unexpected good luck to find herself rid, the police having picked up the jolly monsieur in the course of an unfortunate expedition in the open air. And it was after that arrest that she had come to live in the house in the Rue de La Bruyère, where she had affiliated herself resolutely to the sole confederacy of ladies . . .

"And I thought, privately, that that was the immense history of sapphism, and that no one—no one, you hear—can blame the majority of women fallen into vice, because the male had done everything, and put everything to work, for his pleasure, to distance them from him.

> *Would you like to come, Annaïe,*
> *My beauty.*
> *Would you like to come*
> *Into the fresh air?*

"Latringlette, next door, had started a new song.

"'Oh, will you shut up!' ordered Mina's voice, again.

"'Mina! She's arrived?' my companion put in. 'I didn't hear her come in . . .'

"'Me neither.'

"'What time is it, then?'

"'I don't know.'

"'Don't move. I'll go see.'

"Ida leapt out of bed, went to the window without making a sound, and parted the double curtains gently.

"A pale, livid twilight slid into the room and I read half past five on the clock. And rapidly, thinking that our neighbors might not have drawn the curtains, I peeped through the hole drilled in the wall.

"For once, luck smiled on me; the faded dawn illuminated the room in disorder, where the garments of Jean des Glaïeuls, Gabrielle Mina and Latringlette were lying in piles on the carpet and on the backs of the armchairs. The actress was lying on the bed, the man of joy on a chaise longue and the mariner was sprawled on a goat-skin, with the empty flask of ether tipped over beside him: a sickening tableau of vice and the end of an orgy.

THE END OF THE ORGY
(*Le Supplement*, 13 June 1903)

"THE sickening end of an orgy, in truth, yes—and what a base orgy, devoid of décor: an orgy of the poor, or of Messaline in Suburre! It sickened me, I tell you.

> *We were two, we were three.*
> *We were two, we were three.*
> *Embarked on the Saint-François*
> *Mon tradéri déra*
> *Lon laire.*
> *Mon tradéri déra*
> *Lon la!*

"That Latringlette was becoming decidedly impossible. As Gabrielle Mina had said, he was going to wake the whole house with his bellowing. And the little actress had lavished on him the most energetic appeals: *Shut it! Oh, pack it in! Will you buckle it!* etc., but the drunkard continued braying his sailor's refrains.

"And Jean des Glaïeuls, who was still not budging . . . what a droll effect the orgy had produced on him! He was annihilated, frightfully fatigued—so frightfully that, to put it in popular parlance, you could have fired a cannon next to his ear and I couldn't have guaranteed that he would even have twitched.

"Seeing that she could not obtain anything from Latringlette, and hearing exclamations of anger coming from the corridor and the staircase, Gabrielle Mina decided to employ forceful means. She got up, went to des Glaïeuls, shook him a little, and then more rudely, in order to extract him from his torpor.

The man of joy blinked, stretched himself, and demanded: 'What is it?'

"'It's that your matelot is drunk, completely drunk. You can hear him braying, can't you?'

"'Yes, vaguely.'

"'Vaguely! Well, you've got a strong constitution! He's bellowing like a pig having its throat cut.'

"'What do you expect me to do about it?'

"'It's necessary to make him shut up, or we're going to have disagreements with the neighbors. We're already seen so kindly in the house!'

"'Oh, the opinion of people on my conduct is nothing, absolutely irrelevant, to me. I lead the life I choose to lead. A point, that's all. But if you want to impose silence on Latringlette, I see no inconvenience in it; on the contrary!'

"In fact, Latringlette was howling at the top of his voice:

We're going from Belle-Isle to Groix
We're going from Belle-Isle to Groix,
Come blow, northerly wind
Mon tradéri déra
Lon laire.
Mon tradéri déra
Lon la!

"'Shut up, Latgringlette!' Jean des Glaïeuls tried to put in. 'I beg you!'

"'Go stuff yourself!'

"'It's exactly as if you were preaching in the desert,' murmured Gabrielle, who continued with: 'You can see how he's listening!'

"'The fact is that he doesn't seem to want to answer my prayer!'

"'So?'

"'So, my dear friend, I can only see one thing to do.'

"'What?'

"'Call Mimile and ask him to throw Latringlette out. Only, it's a pity to arrive at that extremity, because that matelot pleases me greatly—oh, very much!—and I wouldn't be sorry to be able to pick him up again, another time . . .'

"'Yes, he's a fine fellow,' Gabrielle agreed. 'But what do you want? We can't attract stories because of him. He's as full as Robespierre's snitch, and full of ether too.'

"'And under that influence, he might keep howling in that fashion for twenty-four hours. You're right. Let's shut him up.'

"Loud voices were audible on the staircase, mostly women's voices, the hoarse voices of nocturnal laborers who needed repose at dawn. There were even a few male voices accompanying them—the voices of clients.'

"'Is that going to finish soon?'

"'What a racket!'

"'One can't sleep!'

"'It's coming from Mina's!'

"'Of course; she's shut in again with a good-for-nothing and her ponce!'

"'What a litany! Great gods, what a chaplet of infamy!'

"And that continued in the house while, still flat on his belly on the goat-skin, the matelot whined:

> *Let's sing to pass the time,*
> *The pleasant amours of a lovely girl,*
> *Who's got the habit of sailors*
> *And has just boarded a ship!*

"Jean des Gläieuls got up.

"'It's necessary to summon Mimile,' he said to Gabrielle, 'in order for him to rid us of that drunkard.'

"But, as if in response, two remarks exchanged by the tenants reached him from the stairwell:

"'If Mimile were here, we could tell him to go up and ask them to shut their mouths!'

"'Yes, but he isn't here; it's his day off. He's gone to bed down with that kid Zizi.'

"'Mimile's not here!' exclaimed Gabrielle. 'Well, we're in the cabbage-patch.'

Latringlette was still howling:

When she saw that her lover was taken,
She changed her clothes right away
And put on a sailor's jersey
And came to sign on to the ship.

"'Listen.' proposed Jean des Glaïeuls, suddenly making a decision. 'We'll have to take him away ourselves, and quickly. They're protesting in the house; there's a storm in the air. I don't want to get beaten up by a gang of fanatical women invading the apartment!'

"'Your bravery is well-known,' mocked Gabrielle.

"'You know full well that I'm as cowardly as a mole,' confessed des Glaïeuls, not without conceit. 'Let's get dressed quickly, put Latringlette's clothes on and get out.'

"'Agreed.'

"And Jean des Glaïeuls, abandoning his sumptuous and ridiculous green peignoir, put on clothes appropriate to his sex. Mina imitated him. That dressing did not take five minutes; the two accomplices were in a hurry, for the people of the house, exasperated by the drunkard's song, were talking serious about coming up or down in order to break down the door.

"The couple was ready to leave; it only remained to dress Latringlette—but that was not an easy task . . . certainly not!

"Oh, that dressing! How difficult it was! First it was necessary to lift the fellow up, establish him in an armchair, put on his socks, his deck-trousers, his woolen chemise, his jacket and his shoes—everything! He did not lend himself to it any more than a cadaver; and Gabrielle Mina and Jean des Glaïeuls, out of breath, were gasping like piano-porters. They bustled around the man feverishly, for fear of the revolution that they sensed taking hold of the whole house; all the female residents and the occasional male guests of the dwelling, exasperated by the howling of Latringlette, the sailor in a crisis of ether, who mortally ill, his face as white as a host, was bellowing his refrains in a veritable fit of *delirium tremens*.

"Oh, that grimacing mouth. contorted into a mask without a drop of blood; and those bulging eyes, which seemed to want to emerge, to leap out of their sockets, and that voice of a furious madman, those precipitate songs, that need to howl and howl again, again and always . . . !

"The dressing was complete now; Jean des Glaïeuls and Gabrielle Mina, exacerbated, could do no more. They launched malevolent gazes at one another, each ready to heap the other with reproaches, bitter words, and more than bitter . . .

"'We have to leave now!' muttered Mina.

"'Hang on,' said des Glaïeuls. 'I've no intention of carrying him to my back. It's necessary to give him the strength to go downstairs.'

"'What are you going to do?'

"'You'll see.'

"He seized the Pravaz syringe, loaded it with morphine and returned to the man.

"'Morphine for that man drunk on ether!' exclaimed Mina. 'You're mad! You'll kill him!'

"'No!'

"'You'll kill him, I tell you; you know that as well as I do.'

"Des Glaïeuls made an ill-tempered movement and replied, dully: 'He'll have strength for a quarter of an hour, perhaps half an hour, That's what he needs; for, I repeat, I have no intention of carrying him downstairs on my back. A drunkard! A boor who might cause me ennuis!'

"'But after that half-hour?'

"'Afterwards? Let him get himself out of trouble. We're going to stick him in a cab downstairs and give no matter what address to the coachman. What will happen will happen. I wash my hands of him.'

"And again, he approached the Pravaz syringe to one of Latringlette's arms, an arm that was hanging inert, the wrist of which was ornamented by a tattoo of a marine anchor.

"'Don't do that!' begged Gabrielle again.

"'And the people of the house, gathering in a mob . . . and this pig, still shouting!' snapped des Glaïeuls, angrily. 'You can see from here how fresh I'll be if the police intervene; my name, my reputation, all that will be soiled because of a drunkard!'

"The man of joy was becoming grossly ignoble . . . ignoble and murderous . . .

"Gabrielle had a hesitation in her revolt; des Glaïeuls took advantage of it, Rapidly, he took the skin of the wretched etheromaniac between two fingers, plunged the needle of the Pravaz syringe into his arm and pushed the whole of its contents into the flesh.

"Then, aided by Gabrielle, unconsciously, he lifted up the drunken sailor, put his beret on his head, and drew him outside, or, rather, dragged him, like a wreck or a bundle of clothes, leaving me terrified by his action.

"Oh, the wretched individual—and how I hated him!

"I heard the sound of footsteps dying away in the stairwell, amid a noise of closing doors, exclamations of contentment and stifled laughter.

"Latringlette had suddenly shut up."

SPIDERS OF THE FORTIFS
(*Le Supplement*, 20 June 1903)

For Liane de Pougy, future Liline[1]

"YES, the matelot had fallen silent, suddenly, and the whole house had become silent again. What had just happened? Had the poor etheromaniac, under the influence of the influx of morphine abruptly injected into him, made the great leap into eternity? No, it could not be that, for Mina and des Glaïeuls—I knew them well—would not have been able to avoid crying their alarm before that death.

"So?

"Feverishly, I got up and hastily put up my hair.

"'You're going?' Ida interrogated, anxiously.

"'Yes, I'm going,'

---

1 Items addressed to Liane de Pougy in the *Supplement*'s gossip columns suggest that "Liline" was a familiar form of address employed by the author with regard to Liane, but give no hint as to its origin. It might not be irrelevant that a character named Liline figures in the Claudine stories, then running as feuilletons in the *Supplement*, credited to Willy but actually the work of Colette.

"'I suspected that you didn't love me!' the strange girl murmured, dolorously and sentimentally. 'You only came for *the other!* And *the other*,' she articulated, almost ferociously, and continued in a hoarse voice: 'That filthy type! But what does he have to do around women, that b*****.' That was another ignominious epithet that you can guess, but which I don't want to pronounce.

"'You'll come back, at least?'

"'Yes, my darling.'

"'Really?'

"'I promise you.'

"'One last kiss, then.'

"'Quickly, for I'm in haste to depart. I need to catch up with them.'

"Ida, her two reptilian arms around my neck, gave me the most ardent, the most passionate of kisses. And I escaped from that chamber of culpable joys, emptied to the marrows, pursued by '*À bientôt, ma chérie, mon amour, ma petite femme,*' etc.—an entire chapter of adorably admiring epithets, so adorably admiring that at any other moment they might perhaps have troubled me, might have created for later a nostalgia of the amorous lesbian's anemic lips.

"That Ida! I've told you that if I live to be a hundred, her face will still be in my memory; that face of the hooker of the crossroads and Montmartre, that hallucinating mask of a strix framed by hair as blonde as ripe wheat, that lustful mouth in which the red pepper of her tongue agitated, quivered and darted!

"The black staircase descended, stumbling—quickly, quickly!—a 'the cordon, if you please' launched through the open door, and I was outside; I found myself on the sidewalk of the Rue de La Bruyère, a Rue de La Bruyère that was still asleep, all the widows closed, and with that, a sharp little wind that suddenly clawed me and made me shiver in my pelisse.

"Mina and des Glaïeuls? Disappeared, vanished, doubtless eclipsed with their prey, that matelot in agony. What to do? Where to go? Where to catch up with them? My thought was adrift, going with the flow.

"I was there, on the edge of the sidewalk, in front of a patisserie whose windows reflected my white and hollow face, with the underside of the eyes outrageously ringed, my hair 'like a mad dog' and my skirt abominably crumpled; I stood there, truly, fearfully stupid, already peered at from the corner of the eye by mocking milkmen perched on their high vehicle, the peaks of their silk caps pulled down over their eyebrows—me, Nine d'Aubusson, whose talent and elegance were celebrated by all the newspapers, on the asphalt of that shady quarter, like a whore hoping for one last client.

"How many minutes did I remain there, sunk in an ocean of unclear reflections, my ears buzzing, fever biting my hands, accelerating my pulse, beating an incessant reveille in my temples, my poor temples, gripped as if by a vice . . . ? Oh, the pain of those awakenings from abominable neurasthenic nights, what atrocious infernos open then!

177

"Yes, that is the hour in which one always pays for the folly of all curiosities! The hour of reckoning . . . and what dolorous debts had I to settle that morning!

"Suddenly, reflections were exchanges alongside me, between two milkmen, who, while lighting a roll-up, had not lost sight of me. The fellows certainly counted on finding a prey in me.

"'You're talking about the Bréda dairy. Oh, I've just seen quite a spectacle there!'

"'Gonzesses *going home* inside?'

"'No, better than that: a kid with two tomcats . . . a matelot who was so drunk he couldn't even let go of a centime . . . and another powdered cove, made up like a whore, with a common streetwalker . . .'

"'I get it . . . what a trio!'

"'You said it, mate. All the same, the matelot had no wind in his sails! The poor fellow! It was almost painful to see a brother of the coast cleaned out like that! And then, he reeked of the pharmacy. It was enough to make a whole regiment of troopers faint . . .'

"'Yes, there are fellows who take too much! Hey, kid in furs, do you want to come and take a glass with us? You have a come-hither mouth that I'd like to stuff . . .'

"It was to me that one of the two men was addressing himself. 'Are you coming? Want a ride?' he continued. 'Very nice, my word—you aren't offered fellows like us every day, so delightful for partying.'

"'Leave off, Firmin,' said the other. 'It's not her who'll let herself fall over this morning. Bonsoir, shepherdess! See you soon, mate.'

"Ironic and grimacing, the two milkmen roused their horses with a whiplash and moved away in opposite directions. And, I, who had just learned, fortuitously, where I could find the three accomplices, headed toward the Rue Breda, and the designated dairy.

"I arrived there five minutes later, but too late to catch up with the trio at whom I had decided to howl their turpitude, and to reproach above all the cruelty of des Glaïeuls, guilty of having morphinated a man under the influence of ether—and what a man! A human rag, rather!

"It was mad, absurd—and also none of my business. But in the state of excitement in which I found myself, I was a little crazy . . .

"'Madame,' one of the girls in the dairy replied to me, 'those people have gone . . . and there was one of them, a sailor, who seemed very ill, poor fellow,'

"'Gone where?'

"'In truth, don't know.'

"'Come on—didn't they say anything.'

"'Wait . . . oh, yes . . . there was the other Monsieur, who mentioned the Quai de Billancourt. Yes, that's where . . .'

"'Exactly,' a nocturnal coachman put in. 'The people Madame is asking about wanted to take me, but in view of the condition of the matelot, I refused. That client scared me!'

"My decision was quickly made. 'What about me, coachman? Are you willing to take me to the Quai de Billancourt?'

179

"'Well, you, Madame, that isn't the same thing. Yes, certainly . . . if there's a good tip.'

"'Here's a louis for the trip.

"'Hop in, then! Cocotte will fly!'

"I installed myself in the fiacre, and in spite of the cold, left one of the windows open, for there was a sickening odor of damp and unwashed sex organs in the carriage.

"And the horse, enlivened by frequent whiplashes, trotted rapidly . . .

"My head, my poor head, was beating the country. It seemed to me that I was racing toward a horrible sabbat, that I was even going toward an atrocious scene of murder. Before my eyes, which closed in spite of my efforts, all the folly of that night of amour and resuscitating poison was evoked. Masks danced before me: that of Ida the street-corner lesbian; that of Gabrielle Mina, des Glaïeuls' procuress; and that of de Glaïeuls himself, the man of joy monstrously coupled with the white, bloodless mask of the matelot.

"Yes, all that danced, danced in smoke, in flames of punch, and the maddening odor of ether arrived at my nostrils . . . and it whirled, intoxicating me with movements, smiles and grimaces that melted again into smiles, so much and so well that my mask, too, was mingled with that extravagance . . .

"A frightful nightmare, a dream of darkness from which I only emerged at an appeal from the coachman. We had arrived at the barrière of Billancourt, between the talus of the fortification and the leaden water; and in the frame of the portière I seemed to perceive, standing out against the gray backcloth of the sky, three silhouettes, two of which were holding up a poor silhouette, collapsed between them, at the extremity of sinew and blood . . .

"Spiders of the fortifs."

THE END OF THE ADVENTURE
(*Le Supplement*, 25 June 1903)

"THE QUAI DE BILLANCOURT at half past six in the morning, the long ocher ribbon of the towpath winding along the edge of the Seine, a Seine in which heavy and curdled water was flowing, a water reminiscent of glue, and in which a flotilla of bateaux-mouches was moored to the bank; the bare fortifs planted with paltry and stunted trees here and there; the customs-post crouching in that woodlouse damp—and above that leprous landscape, which squeezed my heart, a sick sky, steeped in rain, a vast, flat sky, bare and bleak, only stained by the clouds of smoke of the factories of Issy.

"What an atmosphere of murder and abnormal vices reigned there, and how well I understood that it was the only psychic landscape that could suit Jean des Glaïeuls after nights of orgy in the lowest class.

"I had dismissed the coachman and was now walking along the slope of the fortifs in the direction of the miserable trio, a black patch on the desert of the tearful sky—for that Verlainean sky had begun to weep.

It is raining in my heart
As it is raining over the city . . .

"A cold rain that seemed doomed to fall until the culmination of the centuries. The earth was gradually soaked, softening to the point that I had the sensation of walking in moist spiced bread; and sometimes, when I paddled inadvertently in large puddles of water, I also had the impression of placing my feet in liquefied, semi-putrefied things . . .

"It was enough to make one vomit, I tell you.

"And yet, I kept walking, a fever made of indignation, and perhaps curiosity, impelling me toward a terminus that I could not foresee and did not want to foresee.

"Abruptly, the three silhouettes vanished, as if through a trapdoor in a theatrical fantasy, conjured away. I could not retain a cry of amazement. It was so unexpected, so implausible, that disappearance in the midst of the fortifs, so romantic and feuilletonesque, in the fashion of Jean Valjean in *Les Misérables*, worse than that of so many Jules Maryesque or Richebourgian romances.

"In truth, bewildered to the point of going mad, careless of what might happen to me. I picked up my skirts in both hands and went straight ahead . . .

"In less than a quarter of an hour, I arrived at the top of a slope, at the place where it seemed to me that the trio had abruptly sunk into the ground, and I had the explanation of that sudden disappearance: a path descended there steeply, all the way to the Porte Molitor, so steeply that in two strides silhouettes could no longer appear on the horizon.

"I followed that path, and suddenly, a breath like that of a forge reached me . . . a breath from behind a rickety bush. I approached.

"Latringlette was there, lying face up in the mud.

"Oh, those wide eyes—enameled, one might have thought—that drooping jaw, so prodigiously prognathous—but above all, those capsized eyes, of which nothing could any longer be seen but the whites, as if the gaze had risen upwards and was looking 'inside,' into the skull, those eyes of a dead snake in that waxy face! A thin trickle of foam was bubbling at the commissures of the lips. At the ends of the extended and inert arms, the hands, the fingers joined, were rowing, rowing endlessly, with a rhythmic movement. And those were the only indications of life in that frozen body, already almost a cadaver: that panting breath, the bubbling of that foam at the lips, and the cadenced play of those fingers, as if palmate, which were bailing out imaginary water. Those were the death-throes of the big fellow, so solid twelve hours earlier and so cheerful—oh, so cheerful!

"A lightning-flash ripped through my reason . . .

"You see, Fabrice, it's necessary to have lived such moments in order to understand fear . . . abstract fear, supernatural fear, the FEAR that was rising in me . . .

"Fear, the black vulture that was beating its wings beside me and planting its hooked beak in my flesh; FEAR, the hippogriff that was bearing me away. It's necessary for you to imagine that agony at my feet, that living, incarnate nightmare—and my poor head, unhinged by a night of passivity in debauchery, a night during which I had been the victim of that Ida of the sidewalk, the voyeuse of the orgies of des Glaïeuls . . .

"Oh, curiosity punished! Yes, it was the punishment of the daughter of Eve, again!

"I tell you that a lightning-flash ripped through my reason, FEAR was beating its wings in my temples, a vertigo took possession of me, filled my ears with its rumble, widened my eyes, and I seemed to feel them springing out of their sockets; and I too began to row with my hands, as if the mariner's soul were taking possession of mine, as if the fluid of the morphine were bearing me away in its cone of shadow, all the way to Hell . . .

"A struggle was engaged. It was strong, the fellow's astral envelope, it wanted to conquer me, and it conquered me, absorbed me into it . . .

I have drunk your heart!
I have drunk your heart!
I have drunk your heart!

"It was an abominable voice, a treacherous voice of the Beyond, that was buzzing in my ears.

I have drunk your heart!
I have drunk your heart!
I have drunk your heart!

"I uttered a strident scream, which ought to have awakened the heavens, and, rowing with my hands like Latringlette, I slid next to him in the black mud . . .

✳

"The awakening, the house on the water's edge where I found myself, in a low room, reeking of tar and salt, in the depths of a sleazy tavern . . . I was lying on a bed—or a kind of camp-bed—with the winy face of a tavern-keeper beside me . . . and that of Augustine . . . Augustine, my chambermaid . . .

"I had been there for a week, in that corner of Billancourt near to the seductive and treacherous water and its perfidious banks.

"'Yes, Madame,' Augustine explained to me. 'The physician didn't dare to have Madame transported . . . and then, in Madame' position, that would have given rise to talk. Better, wasn't it, that Madame stayed here . . . to cut short any gossip? But Madame can boast of having frightened me. Oh, when the police came to tell me that you had just been found, at eleven o'clock in the morning, in the mud, on the fortifications . . . I couldn't believe it. And yet, it was necessary to agree that it was true, when the papers were shown to me that had been found on Madame, which served to have her identity reconstituted. It was then that I came and took it upon myself to have Madame transported here, close by, chez Gugusse, a good house where the landlord is as mute as a carp. Oh, Madame can say that she's been well cared for in this god-fearing house . . .'

"'Oh, Augustine, I have such a headache!' I exclaimed.

"'Not as much as the Monsieur that was found alongside Madame, I'm sure! Oh, it's not to make reproaches to Madame . . . but Madame will permit me to tell her that that matelot was found more than dead drunk . . . a true cadaver . . . and yet, twenty-four hours later he was on his feet. And he left here without recognizing Madame and saying that he didn't understand it at all . . .'

"'Latringlette? Departed?'

"'Yes, Madame. Well, the commissaire de police, who's a worthy man—Madame should even go to thank him one day, while returning from the races at Auteuil—the watch, as Madame calls it, gave me the advice to have you brought here to avoid a scandal . . .'

"'You did well, Augustine; I can only approve.'

"'All the same,' the worthy girl continued, returning to her idea, 'it's funny that the matelot didn't want to recognize Madame. He left here repeating all the time: *I'm still drunk! I'm still drunk!* Oh, men, aren't they ingrate, Madame, eh?' my chambermaid concluded, shaking her head.

"Needless to say, my dear, two hours later I was at home, my head still aching—that lasted fifteen hours—and cured forever of adventures. Oh yes, forever! So cured of adventures that I never wanted to see Jean des Glaïeuls and Gabrielle Mina again, to whom I forbade my door; des Glaïeuls and La Mina didn't understand and will never understand, that exile.

187

"In any case, I heard shortly afterwards that the couple had split as easily as it had formed; the little actress had departed for Quebec to perform French *chanson* there in a concert tour. As for des Glaïeuls, you won't have forgotten the events that obliged him to leave Paris and France forever . . ."

"And that Ida of the house of a hundred eyes?" I couldn't dispense with asking Nine d'Aubusson. "Have you seen her again?"

"If I had seen her again," replied my friend, smiling and nestling in her bed in the most affected fashion; "if I had seen her again, I wouldn't be waiting for you to join me . . ."

Rosy-fingered dawn, so frequently sung by poets, was making the candlelight pale. On the invitation of Nine d'Aubusson, I untied my cravat, and used my thumb to make my false-collar jump . . .

A PARTIAL LIST OF SNUGGLY BOOKS

G. ALBERT AURIER *Elsewhere and Other Stories*

CHARLES BARBARA *My Lunatic Asylum*

S. HENRY BERTHOUD *Misanthropic Tales*

LÉON BLOY *The Desperate Man*

LÉON BLOY *The Tarantulas' Parlor and Other Unkind Tales*

ÉLÉMIR BOURGES *The Twilight of the Gods*

CYRIEL BUYSSE *The Aunts*

JAMES CHAMPAGNE *Harlem Smoke*

FÉLICIEN CHAMPSAUR *The Latin Orgy*

BRENDAN CONNELL *Unofficial History of Pi Wei*

BRENDAN CONNELL *The Metapheromenoi*

RAFAELA CONTRERAS *The Turquoise Ring and Other Stories*

ADOLFO COUVE *When I Think of My Missing Head*

QUENTIN S. CRISP *Aiaigasa*

LADY DILKE *The Outcast Spirit and Other Stories*

CATHERINE DOUSTEYSSIER-KHOZE
   The Beauty of the Death Cap

ÉDOUARD DUJARDIN *Hauntings*

BERIT ELLINGSEN *Now We Can See the Moon*

ERCKMANN-CHATRIAN *A Malediction*

ALPHONSE ESQUIROS *The Enchanted Castle*

ENRIQUE GÓMEZ CARRILLO *Sentimental Stories*

DELPHI FABRICE *The Red Spider*

EDMOND AND JULES DE GONCOURT *Manette Salomon*

REMY DE GOURMONT *From a Faraway Land*

REMY DE GOURMONT *Morose Vignettes*

GUIDO GOZZANO *Alcina and Other Stories*

GUSTAVE GUICHES *The Modesty of Sodom*

EDWARD HERON-ALLEN *The Complete Shorter Fiction*

EDWARD HERON-ALLEN *Three Ghost-Written Novels*

RHYS HUGHES *Cloud Farming in Wales*

J.-K. HUYSMANS *The Crowds of Lourdes*

J.-K. HUYSMANS *Knapsacks*

COLIN INSOLE *Valerie and Other Stories*

JUSTIN ISIS *Pleasant Tales II*

VICTOR JOLY
The Unknown Collaborator and Other Legendary Tales
MARIE KRYSINSKA *The Path of Amour*
BERNARD LAZARE *The Mirror of Legends*
BERNARD LAZARE *The Torch-Bearers*
MAURICE LEVEL *The Shadow*
JEAN LORRAIN *Errant Vice*
JEAN LORRAIN *Fards and Poisons*
JEAN LORRAIN *Masks in the Tapestry*
JEAN LORRAIN *Monsieur de Bougrelon and Other Stories*
JEAN LORRAIN *Nightmares of an Ether-Drinker*
JEAN LORRAIN *The Soul-Drinker and Other Decadent Fantasies*
ARTHUR MACHEN *N*
ARTHUR MACHEN *Ornaments in Jade*
CAMILLE MAUCLAIR *The Frail Soul and Other Stories*
CATULLE MENDÈS *Bluebirds*
CATULLE MENDÈS *For Reading in the Bath*
CATULLE MENDÈS *Mephistophela*
ÉPHRAÏM MIKHAËL *Halyartes and Other Poems in Prose*
LUIS DE MIRANDA *Who Killed the Poet?*
OCTAVE MIRBEAU *The Death of Balzac*
CHARLES MORICE *Babels, Balloons and Innocent Eyes*
GABRIEL MOUREY *Monada*
DAMIAN MURPHY *Daughters of Apostasy*
KRISTINE ONG MUSLIM *Butterfly Dream*
CHARLES NODIER *Outlaws and Sorrows*
HERSH DOVID NOMBERG *A Cheerful Soul and Other Stories*
PHILOTHÉE O'NEDDY *The Enchanted Ring*
YARROW PAISLEY *Mendicant City*
URSULA PFLUG *Down From*
JEREMY REED *When a Girl Loves a Girl*
JEREMY REED *Bad Boys*
ADOLPHE RETTÉ *Misty Thule*
JEAN RICHEPIN *The Bull-Man and the Grasshopper*
DAVID RIX *A Blast of Hunters*
FREDERICK ROLFE (Baron Corvo) *Amico di Sandro*
JASON ROLFE *An Archive of Human Nonsense*

MARCEL SCHWOB *The Assassins and Other Stories*
MARCEL SCHWOB *Double Heart*
CHRISTIAN HEINRICH SPIESS *The Dwarf of Westerbourg*
BRIAN STABLEFORD (editor)
    Decadence and Symbolism: A Showcase Anthology
BRIAN STABLEFORD (editor) *The Snuggly Satyricon*
BRIAN STABLEFORD (editor) *The Snuggly Satanicon*
BRIAN STABLEFORD *Spirits of the Vasty Deep*
COUNT ERIC STENBOCK *Love, Sleep & Dreams*
COUNT ERIC STENBOCK *Myrtle, Rue & Cypress*
COUNT ERIC STENBOCK *The Shadow of Death*
COUNT ERIC STENBOCK *Studies of Death*
MONTAGUE SUMMERS *The Bride of Christ and Other Fictions*
MONTAGUE SUMMERS *Six Ghost Stories*
GILBERT-AUGUSTIN THIERRY *The Blonde Tress and The Mask*
GILBERT-AUGUSTIN THIERRY *Reincarnation and Redemption*
DOUGLAS THOMPSON *The Fallen West*
TOADHOUSE *Gone Fishing with Samy Rosenstock*
TOADHOUSE *Living and Dying in a Mind Field*
TOADHOUSE *What Makes the Wave Break?*
LÉO TRÉZENIK *Decadent Prose Pieces*
RUGGERO VASARI *Raun*
ILARIE VORONCA *The Confession of a False Soul*
JANE DE LA VAUDÈRE *The Demi-Sexes and The Androgynes*
JANE DE LA VAUDÈRE *The Double Star and Other Occult Fantasies*
JANE DE LA VAUDÈRE *The Mystery of Kama and Brahma's Courtesans*
JANE DE LA VAUDÈRE *The Priestesses of Mylitta*
JANE DE LA VAUDÈRE *Three Flowers and The King of Siam's Amazon*
JANE DE LA VAUDÈRE *The Witch of Ecbatana and The Virgin of Israel*
AUGUSTE VILLIERS DE L'ISLE-ADAM *Isis*
RENÉE VIVIEN AND HÉLÈNE DE ZUYLEN DE NYEVELT
    Faustina and Other Stories
RENÉE VIVIEN *Lilith's Legacy*
RENÉE VIVIEN *A Woman Appeared to Me*
TERESA WILMS MONTT *In the Stillness of Marble*
TERESA WILMS MONTT *Sentimental Doubts*
KAREL VAN DE WOESTIJNE *The Dying Peasant*